A SHIFTER'S SECOND CHANCE

PALE MOONLIGHT, BOOK 3

MARIE JOHNSTON

Years after Gray had a complete mental breakdown that cost him everything, he's clawed his way back to mental balance, a steady job, and a solid relationship with his grown and married daughter. Gone are the years of thinking conspiracies abound and that he is being followed...until a stunning woman busts down his back door and announces that there's a secret world he doesn't know about—and it's hunting him.

After losing her mate and one of her children, Armana abandoned the shifter world to spare the lives of her two surviving children. Two decades later, they're grown and healthy, but she's between packs and still fighting for a relationship with her angry son. So coming to the aid of his mate's human father seems like a good way to prove herself.

Only she can't shake the feelings growing for Gray, and he finds a kindred spirit in her. But if they reach safety, the shifter world won't let Gray keep his memories of their kind. And Armana will become nothing more than a dream that drives him back into insanity.

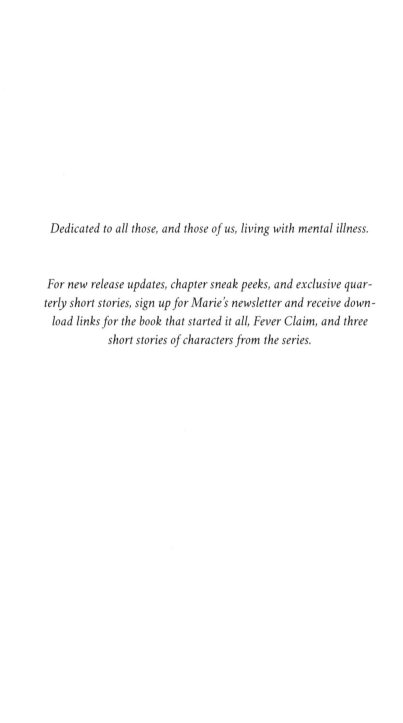

Dedicated to all those, and those of us, living with mental illness.

For new release updates, chapter sneak peeks, and exclusive quarterly short stories, sign up for Marie's newsletter and receive download links for the book that started it all, Fever Claim, and three short stories of characters from the series.

CHAPTER 1

You're going back to the psych ward.

Gray Stockwell snapped the wrinkles out of his plain black shirt and neatly folded it. He set it inside his backpack.

His gaze drifted to the window. *Look outside. They've found you.*

No. He squeezed his eyes shut and summoned his therapist's voice. *No one is after you, Gray. It's the disease talking. No one has found you because no one was looking for you in the first place.*

Dr. Sodhi had been his lifeline for years. That man had seen him through the worst of his disease. When Gray's daughter, Cassie, had been taken away and he'd been committed, Dr. Sodhi had been there. Weeks had bled into months before Gray had been released to live in regular society.

Cassie's lying to you.

"Shut up," Gray snapped at no one. He was alone. There was no one outside watching him. There was no one outside waiting for him.

1

Like Dr. Sodhi said, his concern over his daughter's well-being was natural. She'd gotten married a few years ago and was blissfully happy. It was just that he couldn't visit her in her new home. Neither had he met Jace's mother, a woman who'd been out of Jace's life for years and was now back in it. *She* got to see Cassie's new home.

Cassie and Jace lived in West Creek, across the river from Freemont. Their place was deep in the woods that surrounded the area, amid all the other employees of the security company Jace worked for.

According to Cassie, a lot of families lived there, but they didn't want outsiders to interfere with their training. She'd sent him pictures, but that did little to assuage his fatherly concerns.

What if Jace had tricked her into joining a cult? What if she'd been secretly sold into sexual slavery but was putting on a good show just for him?

But Gray, she still works at the clinic as a psychologist. She wouldn't have her job and meet you for lunch if she was involved in either one of those circumstances.

Thank you, Dr. Sodhi.

Gray glanced down at his task and frowned. He'd packed his clothing into a backpack instead of his dresser.

"Dammit." Fifty damn years old and he was losing his mind. Again.

Those dark years after Lillian had died haunted him. Cassie had been taken away from him and she'd...thrived.

Gray sighed and scratched the back of his neck. They'd taken her away, put her in a new home where she'd met another girl who became as close as a sister. Then Cassie had gone to college, graduated with honors, and gotten her PhD. All because she no longer lived with him.

You don't know what path she would've chosen if she'd stayed with you. She was able to succeed because of the foundation you built.

No, Dr. Sodhi. Because of the foundation *Lillian* had built. His late wife's dogged determination to keep his schizophrenia diagnosis from destroying their family had helped Cassie become the amazing young woman that was his daughter.

Only Lillian had gotten sick and died. He'd gone off his meds in his grief. Cassie had moved on to a new life. And here he was, terrified he was relapsing and would lose her again.

Gritting his teeth, he unpacked his backpack. *No one is following me. Do not listen to the voice in my head.*

And go refill your meds. He couldn't risk running low when his disease was beating against his mental walls.

How long had he functioned like a normal guy? With medication and therapy, he'd rebuilt a relationship with Cassie and was holding down a job at a hunting and camping store, Sporting Warehouse. An unexpected benefit of his off-the-grid living. He had a lot of firsthand knowledge of what equipment worked and what was mediocre or overrated.

Then a few weeks ago he'd seen a dark sedan in his rearview mirror, and it'd tailed him home. He'd pulled into the driveway of his duplex and the car had passed.

The next day, he swore he saw the car again when he was walking into work.

A frantic call to Dr. Sodhi had calmed him. Until Gray saw the sedan again two days later.

Someone new may have moved to the area, and they work in the vicinity of your store. No one is following you, Gray.

Gray went to the window and peeked out.

His heart thudded. Between the blossoming trees of May, across the backyard of the duplex, and on the other side of the street sat that damn car.

Maybe they lived there?

They're following you.

What would Dr. Sodhi say?

Call someone you know is 100 percent real when you have doubts.

Now would be a good time.

He found his phone and dialed Cassie's number.

And he was still staring out the window.

Spinning around, he forced a smile even though Cassie couldn't see it. "Hey, peanut."

"Dad. Everything okay?" She always asked him that. Whether it was automatic or she thought he'd likely *not* be okay, he didn't want to know.

"Yeah. What are your plans this weekend?"

"I was going to plant the garden. My friend Spencer set me up with some seeds and planned a nice plot by the cabin."

"That's great. You want some help?" He couldn't quit trying to invite himself out there. It was the dad in him—he hoped. The disease could be sneaky.

"No, thanks. It'll go fast. Are you sure you're okay?"

"Don't I sound like it?"

"Dad, you sound like you're being falsely chipper."

Talk to your daughter. She's a professional. Dr. Sodhi thought he should have someone to talk to about his mental illness, and Cassie's profession as a psychologist made her an excellent candidate to see signs of deterioration before he hurt himself or others.

But he couldn't bring himself to say it yet. He went with something else that had been bothering him. "It worries me that I can't come out there."

"I know. I'm sorry. And I know it's hard for you to trust me."

So hard. His very nature made secrets more nefarious than they should be. "I don't know what to do with myself this weekend." God, wasn't that the truth. Sit in his apartment and worry about strange men busting through the door? Wonder if the voice in his head was real and his own, or if his paranoia was trying to ruin his life again in the name of self-protection?

No, thanks.

"What's wrong?" Cassie asked.

"Nothing."

"Dad." Cassie's tone said cut the shit. "You don't normally worry about your time off."

"It's nothing. I just… I think I'm seeing things again. Cassie, what if I'm relapsing?"

"You're on your medication, and you haven't missed a dose?"

He wished. That'd explain some things. "No."

"Hallucinations or voices?" Her matter-of-fact way of speaking made it easier to talk about it.

"Both. It started with me seeing a car following me. A black car that'd blend in on the streets or in a president's motorcade. I've seen it a few times. The voices started after that. Well, one voice that says I'm being followed." He snorted. "The car's even parked on the street behind me. Dr. Sodhi's probably right. Someone new moved into the neighborhood."

Cassie didn't reply.

"Peanut?"

"What? No… You've talked to your doctor, good. You know what? Maybe we should get together this weekend. I'll come over tomorrow. 'Kay?"

"I hate to ruin your plans—"

"No. No, Dad, it's fine." Her words came faster. "I'll see you tomorrow. But, you know, call me if anything changes."

"Sure." He laughed. "I'm actually glad I did. It's better that you know what I'm going through."

5

"Seriously, call me. If you think you're being too para-noid, or if— Just call me, Dad."

"Will do. Have a good weekend, peanut." He hung up.

She was worried and he'd caused that. But it'd be worse if he relapsed and no one had a clue it was coming.

* * *

ARMANA MILLER ROCKED in a chair on Jace and Cassie's porch. Sweet Mother Earth, this was one of the most dreadful days she'd had in a long time.

The boredom. It was going to kill her.

She'd lost a mate and a son, barely surviving the mental anguish to raise her remaining two children in secrecy among the humans, only to have both children find their way back to a pack.

And not just any pack. Both of her kids were Guardians, the police force of their kind. In the last couple of years, their role had actually expanded to include both shifters and vampires.

Maggie, the little girl she used to bounce on her knee, was stationed in the colony of her birth with her new mate. The threat to her life had been vanquished and Maggie was living the full shifter life.

And Jace. She'd been estranged from him for so many years in an attempt to keep that threat from touching him or Maggie. They were speaking now, but she questioned her choices every day of her life.

He was standoffish with her, unwilling to trust easily. And she didn't blame him. She deserved it.

But Cassie was welcoming and such a good mate for him.

So her kids were happily mated and working jobs that left Armana fretting for their safety. In the meantime, Armana idled around the main lodge where they let her stay. The cabins were for families and long-term Guardians.

Since the barracks in the expansive lodge weren't completely full, she stayed there. Temporarily. Until they could figure out what to do with her. But the Guardians and their trainees cleaned up after themselves as a lesson in discipline, so there wasn't much for her to do.

She knew nothing about medicine and was therefore no good for helping Doc. Defending herself was one thing, but she didn't know enough to train others.

As the mate of a former colony leader, she was almost useless.

Maybe she should go live in Lobo Springs with Maggie.

A dark cloud smothered her emotions. No. She'd rather not live among the memories of her lost mate and son. That left her with few options. To go back to living in Freemont would be just existing.

Living with the Guardians would have to be enough until she figured out what to do with the rest of her life. A wry chuckle escaped her. She just had to figure out what she wanted to be when she grew up.

Soft squeaks from the chair echoed into the woods where no one was around to hear. At least it was peaceful here.

She let out a long, lingering breath. A run would be nice. Living under the radar meant living just like other humans, and she hadn't been able to indulge her wolf side all those years she'd lived an isolated human life. She hadn't so much as dared to growl. There had been no dating, no social life of any kind, and no thoughts of everything she had lost. She had just concentrated on what she had and tried to keep it.

Cassie banged out the door, phone clutched in her hand. She scanned the woods for a moment before turning. She sucked in a breath but relaxed when Armana smiled. Little things like that reminded Armana that Cassie was truly human, because a shifter would've known as soon as they stepped outside that someone else was there.

"Oh thank goodness. I don't have to go searching for you." Cassie brushed a short brown lock of hair behind her ear. Her shoulders were tense and her posture was rigid.

"What's wrong?" Concern filtered into Armana's awareness.

"I just got off the phone with my dad." She worried her lower lip. "I'm sure it's nothing, but you know his schizophrenia?"

Armana nodded. She hadn't met Gray Stockwell, but Cassie had explained that her dad had mental-health issues.

"He thinks someone's following him." Cassie gave her a small smile. "Ordinarily that would concern me enough, that maybe he's relapsing, but with Jace and his job, I can't help but wonder if he's truly having a hallucination or…"

"Or if he's actually being followed?" Armana couldn't help the thread of excitement that wound through her. Jace was out of town and she couldn't in good conscience allow Cassie to check on her dad in case there was truly trouble.

Cassie pressed her fingertips to her forehead. "I can't even say I'm sure it's nothing. I guess it could be he's noticing someone new in the neighborhood who happens to work near him, too. But I don't believe in coincidences anymore."

"And if it's not a coincidence, then he's either being followed or he's seeing things."

"I have to go check on him."

"No." Armana rose in one smooth motion. Her mind was already working on what she'd need to run to town. "I don't mind an excuse to run to town. Why don't you stay here, and I'll call you if there are any problems? If I don't notice anything, then you'll know he might be relapsing."

"I should really go with you. If he sees you, then he'll

really think that someone is after him, and he's already worried about his mental state."

Armana laughed and brushed her words off. "Oh, he won't see me. I've spent more years sneaking around than he is old. Text me his address and I'll head right there." She jogged down the porch stairs and aimed straight for the lodge.

She reached her room within minutes and dug out clothing that was better suited to spying on someone. Pausing, she stared at the rectangular cedar box on top of her dresser. The ceremonial blade, the *gladdus*, had bonded her to her beloved. How much her life had changed since then. She missed him every day, and her lack of purpose was making it worse.

Shrugging into a long-sleeved black shirt, she considered what weapons she should bring, if any. Being free to be herself again didn't mean that she could shift whenever she felt like it. Discretion meant the survival of their species. But it'd be too hard to dress casually and act normally while hiding a weapon. If Gray was seeing things, then some strange armed woman wouldn't help him.

She stepped into soft black jeans. They were probably too nice for a mission but they'd help her blend. Digging through her closet, she swore as she sifted through her pairs of athletic shoes. Since she'd had to quit working, she'd gotten rid of all her professional clothing, figuring she'd restock her closet with her next identity. She had to be able to blend as a pedestrian or a shopper, whatever the situation required. Finally, she found a pair of black ballet flats. They'd have to do.

What she wouldn't give to have her old leather-soled boots. They were among the many personal items she'd had to ditch when she fled her old pack. Over a century ago, she'd always taken a different route to the lake where her people had gathered their water, and those boots had been ideal for slipping through the woods around the homes of shifters that would give her mate problems.

By doing that, she'd learned which couples were arguing, which were having affairs, and which would, in a disagreement with Bane, either form a united front or solidify a wall of support.

Then she'd had kids, and mates and single pack members confided in her about pack issues, sharing secrets and lowering their guards. Armana saw the real them, their true motivations and fears, and she transferred each tidbit to Bane, who was smart enough to lead in a way that made none the wiser as to her influence. Bane had relied on her eyes and ears to help maintain peace. For all the good it had done him.

But she couldn't deny the thrill coursing down her spine at going out to do something other than pick up a few groceries and run to the bank.

Before she walked out of her room, she grabbed her keys. She hadn't done much driving since moving to the lodge and leaving her job. If her old enemies hadn't come after Maggie, Armana would've had to start a new job soon anyway. Since she looked only thirty-five years old when she was much older than that, she couldn't stay in one place for too long. But she always stayed in Freemont. It had been risky to stay in one city, especially one so close to her old village, but she couldn't bring herself to give up everything again. So she just switched jobs every few years when people started commenting on how young she looked.

Weaving through the compound, she didn't come across anyone. No one would've asked her questions anyway. They were used to her coming and going, but mostly just her hanging around. When she reached the garage she went straight for her car. Her plain tan sedan shouldn't draw any attention from Gray.

Her phone *pinged* with the address. Gray's house was in a part of Freemont that Armana wasn't familiar with, but it should be easy enough to find.

She drove to town. On the way she pondered Gray. Her heart went out to Cassie and the situation with her dad. No matter what Gray's mental state was, they couldn't reveal the other creatures that walked among the humans. Eventually, Gray would also start noticing Cassie wasn't aging. Now that she was mated to Jace, her life span would be equal to his. When one died, so did the other. As shifters, it was hard to survive the death of a mate. Usually the surviving mate died shortly after or went crazy. Or in Armana's case, the shifter had a damn good reason to keep going—like two kids to protect.

She'd wondered, but she'd never asked what Cassie planned to do about her father. Would she risk the wrath of the Guardians and tell him about the presence of shifters, which would also risk his mental stability, or would she and Jace move away? Cassie wasn't the type to fake her own death for her father. And that was too bad.

Armana drove through West Creek and crossed the river into Freemont. Sunset was still a few hours away but the amount of daylight wouldn't matter for her. She could hunt for stalkers night or day.

Tingles drifted through her belly. She wasn't thriving off excitement, was she? Perhaps she'd underestimated her level of boredom.

Gray's area of town was neat. Small, square houses lined the street, tidy yards circled each structure, and any trees were fully mature, forming a canopy over the street. The neighborhood was in an older part of Freemont, but it wasn't an area known for its crime.

First, she meandered through each street of his neighborhood, making sure she didn't go down his street more than once. Then, concentrating on the roads bordering his, she drove slower down each one.

Some houses were quiet, some had cars sitting in the driveway or by the curb, and a few had small children playing outside. She was smiling before she realized it. Nostalgia struck at the oddest times. Those days when her oldest boy had still been alive and all three of her children had played carefree through the village were the best of her life.

After she'd fled with Maggie and Jace, there'd been none of that.

She drove two streets over from Gray's house and parked, making sure that her car wouldn't be visible if he peeked out the windows in the back of his house. She gathered her shoulder-length hair back into a ponytail and secured it. Between her dark clothing and her black hair and the fading sun, she'd be able to roam through all the yards undetected.

As she got out she scented the air. Normal smells like exhaust, lawn chemicals, and cats and dogs were the most obvious. She strolled along the sidewalks first. Just like with driving, she could do one sweep down Gray's street and still be good. By the time she finished canvassing the neighborhood, it'd be twilight and then she could search more thoroughly.

The exuberant sounds of kids playing rang through the neighborhood. Dogs barked, drowning out car engines.

She was rounding the corner to walk up the street behind Gray's house when the smell hit her. Shifter.

It was possible that a shifter lived here. But like Cassie, she didn't believe in coincidences.

Since it would draw suspicion if she abruptly turned around and marched in the opposite direction, she kept going. Relaxing her body so it looked like she was out for an evening stroll, she monitored all the activity around her.

Out of the corner of her eye, Gray's small pale yellow house was visible enough that she could probably look through the windows if she wanted to. And she did. It'd be best if she knew he was home or not first, but she was also insatiably curious about Cassie's father.

Three cars were parked on the road. Only one of them was a nondescript charcoal vehicle, perfect for a would-be stalker. And someone was still inside.

The closer she got to the car, the clearer the driver became. Male, his head reaching the top of the car. He was tall, much like her kind was, and definitely a shifter. His scent grew stronger and more menacing with each foot closer she got.

He would definitely know what she was. Her shifter scent would worm its way through his cracked window. It was what he did about it that would decide how the night would end.

If he left her alone, then she'd assume she hadn't made him suspicious. But if he got out of the car, then he was likely going after her and Gray.

She strode past the guy like she had to get a power walk on, pumping her arms and wiggling her hips like burning calories was the only thing on her mind. She didn't even look inside as she passed.

The engine fired up and the car settled into a soft purr. The male pulled away from the curb and idled to the end of the street. He turned in the direction of Gray's house.

Damn. She waited until he was out of view, then sprinted across the street. Heading straight through the yard behind Gray's, she charged over bushes and fences, hoping no one happened to be looking out the window.

Dogs that had previously been leery about the shifters in

their midst went wild. Ringing barks and throaty growls echoed between the houses, but Armana didn't let that slow her. She leaped over the fence that outlined Gray's yard and ran straight to his back door.

The car was already outside his house.

The back door was locked. She took a deep breath and rammed it open with her shoulder. An older, handsome man sat at a small, square kitchen table with a plate of meatloaf and noodles in front of him. His eyebrows shot up as he stared at Armana.

Sympathy floated through her. The conflict in his eyes said everything. He was trying to decide if she was real or his imagination and whether he should do anything about it either way.

Pounding on the front door made them both flinch.

"Mr. Stockwell, you're in grave danger," a male shouted, probably the other shifter.

"Don't listen to him," Armana said. "You're in danger, but it's from him."

Gray's eyes weren't like his name. They were a warm brown that reflected every emotion he was feeling, and right now he was alarmed and confused.

"Why would that be?" He spoke cautiously, as one would if they didn't know whether they were talking to a vision.

The pounding grew harder until the door shook in its frame.

She had to hurry Gray along. "I'm Jace's mom and Cassie is worried about you. There are things you don't know and I don't have time to explain, but this isn't a hallucination."

At the mention of hallucination, his gaze grew guarded. He slowly stood up, his head swiveling between the door and her. "I have to admit, this is unlike any hallucination I've ever had."

"Like I said, that's because it's not one. Someone's after you and we don't know why. Come with me."

She crossed to him and grabbed him by the bicep. Hard muscle flexed underneath her fingers. The sensation was pleasant, even under these circumstances. More than pleasant. She was tall, like many shifter females, but Gray topped her by a few inches. He wasn't bulging with muscles like a lot of the Guardians, but he obviously took care of himself. Cassie had mentioned he led a regimented lifestyle to minimize his reliance on medication.

The sound of wood splintering propelled her into action. She tugged on Gray and he came easily. She must be less menacing than whoever was at the door.

They were two steps from the back door when the front door was loudly wrenched off its hinges. Gray stopped. "My meds."

Ah hell. If she managed to get him out in time, they'd still have to find a way to get him medication. Coming back to town when he was clearly being hunted wasn't a good idea, at least until they knew why shifters were after him.

She'd have to fight the intruder. Releasing Gray, she instantly missed the loss of his heat. The same male who'd driven the car rushed into the dining room. Their scent led him straight to them.

He bared his fangs in a snarl, and his dark eyes flashed with menace. "Leave us, female. This has nothing to do with you."

"Oh, I disagree," she said sweetly as she advanced toward him.

"Why are you after me?" Gray spoke low but steady.

The male didn't take his gaze off of her. "Don't take it personally, human." The shifter dove for her, his hands outstretched and his fingers curled. Classic shifter move. He intended to wring her neck.

He'd find that wouldn't be so easy. She met him halfway, batting his hands aside and smashing her fist into his face. His shout was filled with pain and surprise. So satisfying. This male was after an innocent man, and it was probably to get to her son.

The shifter recovered quickly and dropped low. They prowled back and forth, but she stayed between the shifter and Gray.

"Do you think you can actually take me, female?" The shifter plucked at her insecurity. He was brawnier than both her and Gray, and he probably lived a life of fighting, and dirty fighting at that.

But she'd been living on pent-up frustration and rage for years, and she'd use every ounce to get Gray safely out of the house. She owed her son and his good-hearted mate that. Just on principle, she had some serious issues with those who targeted humans. They didn't need to be drawn into her people's violence.

The flash of fangs and the bunching of muscles telegraphed the shifter's intentions. She was ready for him. Tucking in low, she met his charge and slammed into him hard enough to propel him backward. A chair clipped her side as she crashed to the floor, but she clenched her jaw and used her fists and knees to keep the male down.

His hands dug into her side, sharp pain flashing through her torso. Rearing back, she brushed a chair with her fingertips. She grabbed it and crashed it atop his head. It wasn't enough to slow him down. He knocked her backward. She landed on her butt with a hard thump.

Fear spiked and for the first time she worried that she wouldn't be enough to take on this shifter. As he was rising, she kicked her foot out and nailed him in the groin. He howled and dropped back to his knees.

She jumped to her feet and intended to keep attacking

him, but a shadow darted around her. Gray swung a black object toward the shifter's head. It hit with a clang that reverberated through the room. The shifter slumped, hitting his face on the floor. He was unconscious.

The impromptu weapon dropped out of Gray's hand and hit the ground with a clatter. A cast iron frying pan. Good choice. She eyed the crumpled form of the male on the floor.

Shifters healed quickly. He'd be back up soon.

"Grab your meds and nothing else, we don't have time," Armana panted. She was breathing like she'd just run ten miles through deep snow. If Gray hadn't stepped in, would she be the one on the floor instead?

Gray stepped over the shifter with a little hop like he was worried the male would grab his ankle. He crossed to a narrow cabinet by the kitchen sink and withdrew a few bottles from inside.

She arched her brow. Only one of those bottles looked prescription. "I certainly hope we didn't delay so you could grab your daily multivitamin."

Gray's solemn gaze considered her. "They are as important to my treatment as my prescription meds."

Whatever. He'd believed her over the other shifter, and he wasn't stopping to question reality. In his case, she wouldn't blame him if he had.

"Come. I'm parked two streets down. I don't know if there's anyone else watching you so stay alert." She opened the back door. Flakes of paint and bits of wood fluttered to the floor from when she had barged in. Smelling the air and listening for anything unusual, she motioned for Gray to follow her.

He hugged his bottles to his chest with one hand, and even though her back was to him, she swore his gaze caressed her whenever he looked at her. Foolish. She'd been alone too long and this was Cassie's dad and they were both in danger without knowing from whom or why. Amorous thoughts had no business in her head right now.

They reached the fence and she slowed. She wouldn't think twice about jumping it. It was like stepping over a pebble in her path, but for Gray it was a four-foot fence.

She scanned the length of the chain-link. There had to be a gate. No luck. It was a stretch of fence that completed the enclosure of his yard by connecting to the fences that ran parallel on either side.

"I can help you over." She assessed him, thinking she could just offer her clasped hands for him to use as a step.

"I can hop over and then help you," he offered.

"No. Just chalk up what you see next as evidence of the new world we're going to tell you about." She sprang over the top and landed in a crouch on the other side. She turned to gauge his reaction.

Gray's lips parted and his brows crept toward his hairline. For a human male, he had a full head of hair. An attractive salt-and-pepper look, but heavier on the pepper. His rich brown hair was several shades deeper than Cassie's.

Cassie must have looked more like her mother, but her resemblance to her father was more than physical. Gray had a calm and collected demeanor, much like his daughter. The way they stood and watched the world before deciding how to react was almost identical.

Gray didn't say a word. It was like he gave himself over to the hallucination, deciding not to care anymore if it was real or fake.

He handed his bottles over to her. One was indeed a prescription bottle, another was a multivitamin, and the third was some sort of B vitamin. If he said he needed them, then she believed him. It wasn't like Cassie to exaggerate what had happened to him when she was younger. And if he was stable enough to own his own home and treat himself, then these bottles were probably his lifeline.

Propping both his hands on top of the fence, he launched himself over, clearing it neatly and sticking a solid landing. Seeing firsthand the bunch of his muscles and the confidence with which he carried himself, Armana shouldn't have been surprised. She didn't often see a human of his age in such prime shape. She hadn't paid attention to any of them.

He held his hands out to accept the bottles back, careful not to touch her. Their gazes met for a brief second before he dropped his to his pills. "What is this new world you mentioned?"

"I'm sure your fatherly intuition made it seem like Cassie was hiding things, yeah?" When he nodded, she said, "That's because she is."

His gaze darkened. "Is she all right?" His body snapped with tension. The idea of his daughter being in danger made him almost as menacing as the shifter he'd knocked out.

"She is. And I'm glad I told her not to come tonight. She's worried you're either relapsing or truly being followed." Armana lifted a shoulder and kept her voice light. "And now I guess we know."

She took off across his back neighbor's yard, and he followed. The sun had sunk farther and it was officially twilight. Perfect. He might not be able to see as well as she could, but as long as they stuck together he'd be fine and they wouldn't be as visible to the residents.

Dogs picked up their barking, but there was nothing she could do about it. It wasn't as frantic as when the male had roamed with ill intentions. She couldn't communicate with dogs, but they could sense her nature.

She picked her way through the lawn until they reached the front. They strode side by side along the sidewalk until they reached the car. He slid into the passenger seat without question.

"So are you gonna tell me about Cassie's secret life or will she?"

Good question. Armana had never needed to reveal the existence of her kind to a human before, and it wasn't a task she relished. Humans were an unpredictable bunch. They could panic and raze anything they feared, or they could embrace it and champion its cause. In this day and age, humans accepted the strange more readily than they used to. They almost relished it. The goth phase had even taken vampires by surprise.

But Gray was older. He may not have been a young kid raised on stories of mythical aliens and vampires and were-wolves. Then there was the fact that the new species she was going to inform him about threatened his daughter. And that his daughter had married one. Mated with one. That would be a new concept for him, too.

"I think it's best if Cassie tells you herself."

He nodded and stared out the passenger window. "I'll accept it better from her. I know she's real. Her voice always trumps the ones in my head."

"Have you been hearing voices, too, ones that you haven't heard before?" She was prying, but just like the strange male, she had to rule out any outside forces interfering in Gray's life. Shifters couldn't normally communicate telepathically with humans, but they often had special abilities, so she couldn't rule it out. She doubted vampires were messing with him in the way they did when they mesmerized their meals. Gray didn't smell anemic and she scented no fangers on him.

Gray scowled. "How much do you know about me and my problems?"

"As much as you'll learn about me once you are brought

up to speed with our world." Her past wasn't a secret. It was a tragedy used as an example to other villages about what could happen during an uprising, and how one mate could find the will to go on after losing the love of her life.

"I don't even know your name. Only that you claim to be Jace's mother, but you look like you could be his sister."

"My life span is much longer than yours. Rest assured I'm old enough to be his mother."

"Life span? No voices have ever spoken as crazy as you." He laughed without humor. "That means you must be real."

"I am."

They drove in silence. A few times, Gray pried his gaze away from the window and glanced at her. Whenever his eyes landed on her, a warm glow spread through her body. It had to be the aftereffects of the adrenaline.

She was a widow and a mother. That had been her identity for so long, she didn't know anything different.

She glanced in the rearview mirror. Well, damn. They had company.

CHAPTER 2

*G*ray swallowed hard. The woman next to him clenched her hand around the steering wheel, and the corners of her eyes pinched as she squinted into the rearview mirror.

He ducked his head to peek into the side mirror. It wasn't long before he picked out two dark vehicles weaving through traffic to stay behind them.

"We're being followed." He didn't have to ask. The behavior of the cars was so obvious that he didn't question what he was seeing.

He should be questioning much more about the night, but it all seemed too real. The sights, the smells, the striking beauty of the woman next to him, it was all unlike any hallucination he'd experienced before. And, he feared, that was because it was reality.

Cassie was in danger.

He wanted to demand answers from Jace's mom, but she was right. He would have a hard time believing anything she said. When it came from Cassie's mouth, he'd be able to believe.

He might need to schedule another session with his doc, though.

"The people who are after you are certainly determined." She increased her speed and took the next two sharp rights. If it weren't for the tightness in her jaw, and the white knuckles around the steering wheel, he wouldn't have known she was concerned. She drove steadily and kept her actions from drawing attention.

"Just tell me one thing. Is Cassie safe with Jace?" Because none of the rest mattered—the hallucinations, the voices, the man busting into his house, none of it. His main priority would always be his daughter's safety.

Sometimes his disease fooled him about whether her life was truly in danger. The worst was after Lillian had died and he'd thought the government was spying on him. He'd uprooted her and they'd lived off the grid. A young girl missing school because her dad was delusional. Her safety was paramount, but he had to distinguish between real danger and his disease.

Jace's mom pinned him with her vivid blue gaze. It was clear where her son had gotten his icy-blue eyes. "My boy would give his life for her. But he shouldn't need to, because he's one of the most excellent fighters I've ever known. He got that from his father," she murmured.

According to Cassie, Jace had lost his dad and brother years ago. But pain still rang in this woman's voice. It must be how he sounded when he mentioned his late wife.

"I never did get your name," he said. "I'm Gray Stockwell."

The corner of her mouth worked. "Armana Troye—Miller. Well, my real last name is Troye, but I've been going by Miller since I lost my ma—husband."

Was it his imagination or did a fleeting look of guilt cross her face? "It sounds like there's a story there, too."

"We all have stories. Not all of us get happy endings, but oh, do we have stories. It's the life of my kind, I guess."

"Is your kind different from that man that broke into my house?" The direction of this conversation was surreal. He should be questioning himself more than he was. He should already have his doctor's number dialed and the phone to his ear.

Her mouth flattened in a hard line. "Unfortunately, we are the same."

Gray went back to staring out the window and peering into the side mirror. A black sedan was still on their tail.

"I see it," Armana said. "If I can't lose him, we may be forced to choose a different route back to Cassie."

"Which would be?" All he knew was that Cassie lived outside of West Creek. What other route could they take to her? Boat? She hadn't mentioned living that close to the river.

"On foot through the woods, and with you that would be a serious disadvantage."

He tensed and squeezed his eyes shut. Running for his life through the woods only brought back unhappy memories. For years he'd clung to the time he got to spend with Cassie before she was taken away, but he'd never forgotten the reason they were out there in the first place. He did his best to avoid remembering, lest he return to that dark mental place he'd been in after Lillian had died.

"What's wrong?" Armana asked sharply. "Can you run? Are you afraid of the woods?"

"No, I'm much too comfortable there." The call to live off the grid had been like a siren song. It was hard to think of a wilderness hike and not worry his paranoia would return. His tendency toward isolation was bad enough.

He'd never made friends easily. The nature of his disease made it hard for him to trust. After Cassie had been put into foster care, he'd concentrated on healing himself to get her back. By the time that had happened, she'd been an adult and his priority had been building a relationship with her. Now she lived out of town, and they only got together a few times a month, nothing more than an hour or two for lunch or dinner.

The extent of his life was work and home. To break things up, he had a gym membership and went for runs— within city limits. He kept his coworkers at arm's length because he didn't want to share any of his past with them. It was refreshing to be thought of as just a normal guy.

"You make it sound bad," Armana said. "But I assure you, any advantage you can give us will help us reach Cassie alive."

"Perhaps I should've pressed for more of the story," he muttered. Still didn't matter, though. He had his medication, Armana said Cassie was safe for the moment, and he could do nothing about his past. All he needed to concentrate on was getting to Cassie without leading these people to her doorstep.

Dammit. He hadn't grabbed his phone as he was running out. He should call Cassie to verify that Armana was who she said she was.

"Do you have a phone?" he asked.

She shot him another stare that rivaled her son's glacial gaze. "Why?"

He went with honesty. "I should verify who you are."

She tapped the console but kept her eyes on the road. That boded well, but at the same time it didn't make him feel better. Part of him hoped he was the only one wrapped up in a situation of his mind's making. But that she was willing to let him call Cassie meant that his daughter was embroiled in this as well.

He dug out her phone and dialed Cassie's number. When

she answered he couldn't find words or think of what he should say.

Armana plucked the phone out of his hand. "Yes, Cassie. Your father wasn't hallucinating. We are on our way but we're being followed." She paused. "Shifter. No. You stay right where you're at. It won't do either of us any good if he has to worry about you. Can you reassure him about who I am?" Armana handed the phone back.

He stared at it for a heartbeat before putting it to his ear. "Peanut?"

"I'm really sorry, Dad." His daughter's voice was a relief. "I can explain everything when you get here, but I need you to listen to Armana and get here safely."

"You know who these people following us are?" It would make him feel better to know their identity. He had no weapons—he was lucky he'd left the house with his shoes on —and this wasn't his vehicle. Information was his best advantage.

"They aren't like you and I. They're like Jace and his mom, and all the people Jace works with. Most of them, anyway. Can you do what Armana says?"

Meaning could he hold it together and not run away, thinking the government was after him? He took a quick inventory of himself. Despite the uncertainty of the last few days when he'd been plagued with anxiety about a relapse, he felt complete, whole. Healthy inside and out.

"Yes, but only for you," he said.

"Dad...you're going to find out things that will blow your mind but hang in there. Please." The worry that infused that last word broke his heart. He'd caused that.

"Can these people get to you where you're at?"

Cassie's hard laugh was one he hadn't heard from her before. "One, they'd sorely regret it if they tried. Two, I suspect they're after you because they can't get to me here, or get to Jace anywhere."

Armana held her hand out and waggled her fingers. Gray frowned at them, but she lifted her chin toward the phone. Oh.

"Love you to the moon and back, peanut. Armana needs to talk to you again."

Armana took the phone. "Have you talked to Jace?" Pause. "I will talk to him first. Any details I can find out, the better." She handed the phone back to him. "Look for Jace in my contacts and call him."

She steered over the bridge into West Creek. If they were going to have to make a run for it, she'd be stopping soon. Gray slowly inhaled, counted to four, held it for a second, and released while counting to four again. He found Jace's name and hit dial. Armana snatched it out of his hand and put it to her ear.

He switched his concentration to their surroundings. Back into the woods. A place he had avoided. They were still inside city limits, but he dreaded the moment he was surrounded by trees again. What if they were a trigger for him and brought back the voices telling him he needed to run, to save himself and his daughter? In this situation, it'd hit too close to the truth.

Armana's lilting words invaded his thoughts. She had a nice voice, strong and confident. He shook his head. This wasn't the time to notice such things.

She rattled off what had happened, from Cassie's anxiety after their talk to the man in his house to where they were now. She said the word *shifter* again. What did that mean?

"Any ideas who they are and what we're up against?" Her gaze flicked from the rearview mirror to the road stretching in front of them. Just when he thought she'd keep going straight out of town, she took a right. Their pursuers hung back. They had to know they'd been spotted. Were they trying to avoid being seen, or were they messing with his and Armana's minds?

Armana ended the call and tucked the phone into her pants pocket. Her black jeans molded themselves to every curve; it was a marvel that her phone could fit.

"Did Jace have any information?" *And how are you old enough to be his mother?* Not one line marked her face, but there were hints around her eyes that if she smiled they would crease as her eyes twinkled.

He'd love to see her smile.

No. He swiveled his gaze back out the passenger window. He missed his wife and he was lonely, but that was no excuse for dwelling on how beautiful Armana was. His daughter was married to her son.

"Jace is like a police officer for our people." Armana took a left and then another quick left. He doubted it would help. Before her first left, he spotted the car. "He said he's been working on a case involving human trafficking. The males involved are especially crafty and brutal. And greedy." She glanced at him. "There's a lot of money in the flesh trade."

"And he's getting too close, so the guys he's after want to steal his woman?"

Armana nodded, her features tight. "An eye for an eye. He stole product from them, so they'll steal what they can back."

Jace is like a police officer. Cassie had described his profession in a similar way but more like security. "If Jace isn't a police officer, then what is he? Is he a federal agent, is that why you're all secretive?" Is that what they meant by *our kind*?

"He is all of them rolled into one. We aren't like you. We can't be policed in the way humans are."

"You keep referring to humans. What are you?" He

couldn't hide the rise of his temper; it lashed out with his words.

She blew out a gusty breath. "Fine. We're shifters."

"Shifters of what?"

"Into a wolf." She yanked the wheel to the right and he had to grab the *oh shit* handle before he slammed into the door.

"Shift…into a wolf?" It didn't make sense.

"You'll see soon enough." She stomped on the gas. Residential buildings turned into blue-collar businesses. Service centers. Storage units. Fly-by-night auto sales. They were heading out of town. "Our life spans are longer, much longer. That's why I don't look much older than Jace, but I am. We are also wilder, more savage. No matter how civilized the rest of the world gets, we can't outrun our nature. We live in hiding as much as possible, and people like Jace protect us from humans, humans from us, and us from each other."

She didn't sound crazy, and Cassie wasn't the type to reside with people who lived in a delusion. He tried to buy into it, but he couldn't.

"How much longer do you live?" It seemed like the simplest question he could ask.

"Centuries."

Well, that was hard to believe. "So you're saying that Jace will outlive Cassie by centuries?"

"No, their souls are linked together. When one dies, the other dies."

"Bullshit." On top of worrying about Cassie, he couldn't worry about Jace and that his death would steal Cassie away. What she described wasn't possible.

Their speed crept higher. Trees were closing in around them on either side of the road. His lungs constricted and he squeezed his fists.

It was just a drive; it didn't mean he was going back in time.

"Not that I wouldn't be working to keep Cassie safe, but you can imagine that getting to her would solve the traffickers' problems with Jace several ways."

"And these people after us are shifters?"

"Some of the nastiest. And that's saying a lot."

"Is there anyone else they can go after?" If he bought their story, it would make sense that Cassie was a target. But why him? Whatever the reason, he was oddly grateful. Because that meant they couldn't get to his daughter.

"Shifters don't mate with humans very often. We prefer to live in villages, surrounded by our own kind. But because of our past, Jace was raised in the human world." She lifted her shoulder. "Which turned out well I guess, since his mate is human. But he is a Guardian and those he's after will target any weak points. Cassie would be his weakness, but she's surrounded by other Guardians, so that leaves you."

If all this was true, the way Cassie had been acting since she had met Jace made sense. How could it be true? It was absurd.

Absurd or not, he was on the run and he couldn't lead them back to Cassie. He glared at the trees around him. He was not his past self. He was strong, and he was as mentally sound as he could get. The woods would not trigger him.

Cassie's lying to you.

He squeezed his eyes shut for a heartbeat and opened them. He had reconciled that he was fully immersed in reality, but now the voices taunted him. Was his indecision prompting them?

Did it matter? He had to get to Cassie. He'd deal with the rest later.

CHAPTER 3

*A*rmana had taken the highway out of town on the opposite end of West Creek from where the Guardian lodge was. She'd needed time to formulate a plan. She had to shed her clothes, shift, and keep Gray from losing his shit when he saw her turn into a wolf. That would be hard for any human to take, much less one with his history.

Gray was handling all of this quite well. She'd love to listen to his thoughts. Was he still deciding whether he should believe her or not? Was he planning to bolt as soon as she stopped the car? Because that would endanger both of them if she had to chase after him while evading the shifters following them.

She might as well ask him and sniff out whether he was lying or not. Then she'd know if she had to prepare to chase after him. "You're handling this quite well."

"There is no other way to handle this. I have to get to Cassie. I've seen the evidence myself that someone's after me, and you seem like the best way to keep danger from her doorstep."

He smelled sincere. His scent was fresh and clean, like the

first few minutes after a summer rain. She missed those times when she'd frolic in the meadow after a thunderstorm. Once the kids had come along, she and Bane hadn't had many opportunities, but when they'd run together, they'd made those moments count.

Being chased wasn't the time to remember the good times, the carefree moments in the years before death knocked on her door. And doing so after admiring how good Gray looked and smelled seemed inappropriate. The word "sexy" hovered on the edge of her mind and she had no business thinking about Gray like that.

Gray sounded calm and collected now, but what would he do when she sprouted fur?

She turned off the highway onto a dirt road and floored it. Rocks sprayed up from the rear wheels. The dust cloud wouldn't hide them, but she had to make her way as close to Guardian land as she could get. The shorter the distance Gray had to run, the better their chances.

Gray gripped the dashboard and clenched a fist around the handle attached to the roof as she stomped on the brakes to turn and then sped up again. During her downtimes, she'd had nothing to do but run these woods, but she hadn't gone out as often as she should've. By now, she should've known this land just as well as she had known her old village.

She couldn't see the car behind her anymore, but that didn't mean he wasn't there. It also didn't mean that he hadn't called in reinforcements.

She turned onto a county maintenance road that was nothing more than two parallel lines worn in the grass that wound between the trees. The car bumped along and the pills clattered in Gray's bottles. He released the dash to scoop up the meds and hug them to his chest.

The trees were getting closer together and the foliage thicker. She found a spot where the underbrush grew high but where she could wedge the car between a couple trees and still be able to open the doors.

As soon as she parked and killed the engine, she got out and Gray did the same. She didn't waste any time. Her shirt came off first, then she kicked off her ballet flats and peeled down her pants.

"What are you...?"

She glanced over at a slack-jawed Gray. He stood holding the pill bottles to his chest just like he had in the car. He averted his eyes as if to give her a measure of privacy. He would also learn that her kind wasn't discreet.

"Like I said, I'm going to turn into a wolf, you're going to run as fast as you can after me, and we're going to desperately hope that we make it to the Guardians in time."

He'd have to see to believe. She envisioned her wolf and flowed into her other form.

His choked gasp was loud to her sensitive ears. "Oh my God, what just happened?"

She swiveled around so he could look her in the eye and see that it was still her—her eyes, with her hair coloring, just on four legs and with a snout. If only she could speak to him telepathically, but that didn't work with humans.

He wasn't looking at her. He blinked at the bottles in his hand.

She trotted to him and circled around in hopes that he understood they had to get going.

Darting ahead several feet, she went in the direction they needed to run and stopped. He still hadn't moved, and he still wasn't looking at her.

She gave a soft bark. He flinched and cast a dumbfounded stare her way.

Well, at least he was looking at her now. But he didn't move.

She flowed back to her human form. "You have to run after me or they'll catch you."

He jerked his gaze away and shook his head. "You're naked."

"Because clothing gets tangled in my legs. My kind isn't embarrassed about our bodies. I'm shifting back and you must follow me."

He was shaking his head again and avoiding her gaze.

She stomped over to him, grabbed his collar, and leaned in. "You must follow me. For Cassie."

He finally looked at her. His eyes filled with resolve. He dipped his head and readjusted his bottles.

She transitioned into her wolf and took off. Every few yards she checked over her shoulder to see how he was doing. Extraordinarily well for a human. Had he spent time in the woods? She remembered Cassie saying something about camping with her dad for a long period of time, which he'd gotten into trouble for, but Cassie didn't talk about her childhood often.

Gray hopped over felled tree limbs and adjusted his course with each step, all without tripping or falling.

She let her tongue loll out with exhilaration. If Gray could sustain a run like this, they were going to make it. It was only a couple of miles to Guardian property, where the perimeter would be protected. Whoever was monitoring security would see them and let them in, but any pursuers would be stuck outside the warded boundary.

Zigzagging through trees and around limbs, she chose a path based on Gray's abilities. She bypassed several ideal spots that she could slip through because Gray would require too much time to crawl through.

Minutes ticked by, the occasional howl interspersed with Gray's measured breathing and grunts of effort. They'd only gone a few hundred yards. Her optimism faltered. What if he couldn't sustain this pace? This was difficult terrain for a human to hike through, much less sprint.

Armana's lungs began to burn more with each hill. She continued to glance back. Gray was falling back farther each time. Fatigue was weighing on him.

She was tiring far sooner than she should've, and she couldn't blame it on the stress of getting caught. She'd let herself go in the last two decades that she'd hidden among the humans. A swirl of shame wove through her. The most basic part of her had been taken for granted. She'd always assumed that she could keep her son and daughter safe because she was a shifter, born and raised.

She had. Sort of. Maggie had almost gotten captured and killed because she hadn't been familiar with her shifter side. Jace had done hard time to protect Maggie, and Armana had cut herself off from him to protect Maggie.

Funny how a flight for her life could send a steady stream of regrets running through her mind like an old-time film.

Armana should've been there for Jace. She should've introduced Maggie to her wolf long before her life was threatened. She should've done a few workouts of her own. Her innate nature needed to be exercised as often as her regular body. Obviously, Gray hadn't slacked on his exercise.

She gauged his progress. He was dropping behind.

Howls rang in the distance. The sounds were getting closer. She counted at least three different wolves chasing them. How many more were out there that were remaining quiet in order to sneak up on them?

She cleared a ridge and skidded to a stop. The other side was a craggy drop-off with exposed roots, almost like the hill had been cut in half. No matter how agile Gray was, he wasn't going to be able to clear that without breaking bones. She trotted along the ridgeline as Gray approached. His breathing was heavy, and his forehead was slicked with sweat that dripped onto his T-shirt. The exertion was wearing on him.

"Yeah, I can't jump that," he panted.

Barks mingled with the howls. The other shifters were communicating with each other.

Had they planned this? Did they know the terrain well enough to have steered them into the side of a cliff?

The ridge sloped downward but took them farther from the Guardian's property. Tracing it the other direction would only close the distance between them and their pursuers.

Her head jerked up as a new set of howls echoed from the opposite direction. The howls were nothing different than a regular wolf's, or a dog's. Shifters communicated telepathically. Interpreting them would be the same as interpreting a sigh. Context was everything. She assumed these new howls were because they were in on the hunt.

What if they were using code, a special dialect of howl that only they understood?

The very thought left a cold sense of danger lingering inside of her. They weren't just rogue beasts hell-bent on revenge. If they were determined, manipulative, and cunning, then Armana and Gray stood very little chance of reaching the lodge safely.

What had their plan for the night been? Had they assumed Cassie and Jace had broken sacred rules and told Gray about their kind and they could torture the information out of him? Had they expected Gray to flee to the lodge and they would follow?

Or had she interfered and gotten themselves circled because they'd called more shifters? Without her, they would've taken him and questioned him or used him as bait, but it would've left an opening for the commander of the Guardians to mount a response and rescue him.

Understanding dawned on Gray. His eyes widened and he swiveled his head to look in each direction.

"Do we head the way we came?"

She shook her shaggy head. No, if her car had been found, they'd have someone monitoring it. They needed help.

Her mind spun through a list of names to call to telepathically. Her son was away on a mission. Cassie wouldn't be able to hear her thoughts. And she didn't know many of the other shifters well enough, but Commander Fitzsimmons was always around and always on duty.

We need help at the southern perimeter.

Had Cassie already talked to the commander about their situation? Either way, he was going to find out that rogue shifters were a threat to the lodge and its occupants.

I have a human with me and we need help.

"Where exactly do we need to go?" Gray glanced at her and then scanned around like it was ridiculous to be talking to a dog. Their situation was dire or her hackles would've risen. He'd adapted and adjusted, she couldn't take it personally.

She padded toward him and lifted her nose in the direction of the lodge, which was still over a mile away on the other side of the rocky crag. There was a good reason the southern perimeter of the lodge butted up against this formation of the earth: natural protection. The wards of the perimeter stretched like an invisible wall, rising up high enough that she couldn't jump over them, and both of them would receive a hell of a shock if they came into contact with the wards.

As the sounds of the wolves drew closer, Armana was struck with a monumental sense of failure. She had failed her son, and it was only out of Jace's sheer will, intelligence, and strength that he'd managed to pull himself out of the gutter he'd landed in.

"Can you get down that?" Gray pointed over the edge, his keen look calculating a path down.

A male's firm voice filtered into her mind. *We're already on our way.*

Welcome relief brought her back from the edge of despair. The Guardians' security had picked up on the danger and were en route.

She gave Gray an exaggerated nod to make it obvious. She would skid and tumble, but she could reach the bottom without injuring herself. The major problem was that the rogue shifters might have known about this spot and winged around it while intentionally running her and Gray into it.

She flowed out of her wolf form and planted her hands on her hips.

He cleared his throat and spun away, but not before she caught the flash of heat in his eyes.

He was attracted to her. But not only was this the wrong time, he was also human and Cassie's dad.

Armana wouldn't earn Jace's forgiveness if she so much as mentioned Cassie's dad was the first male to turn her head in years.

She focused on their plight. "I can get down. You might break a bone, and that would put a serious kink in our plans. Commander Fitzsimmons is on the way with help."

"Who?" His shoulders were tight, but his breathing had slowed. They'd been standing here too long.

"Jace's boss."

"Shifter?"

"Yes. It's daylight so no vampires can come to our aid."

He spun. "Vampires?" His gaze raked her body. She didn't look down, but a hot flush crept up her torso. He caught himself and turned around again.

"Dammit, Gray, this isn't the time for modesty," she

snapped. "Yes, vampires. They drink blood. We turn into wolves. We've been around almost as long as humans."

He didn't respond to the vampire comment but cocked his head. "They haven't howled in a while."

She stilled. They hadn't. She sniffed the air. He craned his head around, disbelief in his gaze.

She shot him a glare. "I'm sniffing for them, and I don't smell them."

He pointed in the direction the new howls had come from. "Maybe the new ones over there gave them a signal to give up."

"Rogue shifters don't give up so easily. If they did, there was a damn good reason."

"Rogue shifters now?"

She nearly growled, but she stuffed her frustration back and put herself in his place. What if someone told her that no, Santa Claus was the real deal? The tooth fairy? And what was the other tradition Maggie had conned her into doing? That's right—the Easter Bunny.

Concentrating on seeing as far into the trees as possible, she scented the air again and recoiled. Gray jerked his head around.

"Smoke," she said. "Fire. They set the woods on fire."

An explosion made the leaves shake on the trees. She jumped, landing closer to Gray. He automatically clasped an arm around her waist but released her immediately.

"I can smell it now. Where's it coming from?"

She shook her head. "It's everywhere. This was a normal year for rain, it's not that dry. They must've used an accelerant."

"That might've been your car that blew."

"And here I just paid it off."

He flashed her a smile, rooting her in place.

The short lines that fanned from the corner of his eyes

only added to his looks. His brown eyes sparkled, if only for a moment, and lightened to the rich color of polished oak.

She tore her gaze away from him and peeked over the ridge. "They can't have surrounded us because of the wards. They may have circled us in, but it would only be a half circle."

"So we go down. You'd better...uh...shift."

She lifted a brow before she transitioned. Stretching on her haunches, she envisioned the jump. Crouching low, she leaped, aiming for an area with a slope a few degrees shallower than the rest of the side.

As she landed, her weight propelled her forward and she went with it, instinct kicking in as she bounded down. She trotted to a stop at the bottom, where it gently swelled into a larger hill that hopefully wasn't eroded away.

Gray was already on his way down, his belly pressed to the ground, maintaining three points of contact. He was stretched over the edge, his fingertips slipping from the roots and dirt they dug into. Just when she thought he'd plummet, he let go and used his feet as both a guide and a brake.

He managed to stop after several feet. Haze was filling the air. Whatever they'd used to start the fire had done a stellar job. A blaze raged toward them.

Gray dropped again. He was skidding to the bottom. Flinging his hands out to gain purchase on something, he flailed at air. He hit the bottom and cartwheeled to the side to catch himself. She winced at the thud he made.

Had he hurt himself? If he had, they might not be able to outrun the fire to get to safety. He stayed in a crumpled heap, the only sound coming from him a low moan.

CHAPTER 4

*G*ray planted his hands and pushed against the earth. He grunted to his knees. The wolf prodded his side. He wanted to snap, *yeah, yeah, I know,* but after her amazing show of agility, he felt like a clumsy toddler who'd challenged a flight of stairs and lost.

His ribs hurt, but it was superficial, scrapes from where he'd abraded layers of skin off his abdomen and side.

It was the landing, though. That was when something had popped in his ankle and pain had flared in the familiar way of a sprain.

The wolf—Armana. Could he get used to calling what was clearly an abnormally large wolf by the name of a female with the body of a centerfold?

Armana whined again.

His world shrank as he spotted his scattered pill bottles. Scrambling through the dirt and weeds, he swept the bottles toward him. They'd stayed shut. Thank God.

He wasn't going to endanger anyone because they had to go to town to refill his meds. He hated being a burden on society and his loved ones. But he'd gotten hurt and Armana probably wasn't going to get herself to safety without him. If she hadn't ditched him yet, it wasn't happening.

He knew almost nothing about her, hadn't yet reconciled what he'd seen with reality, but his respect for her grew.

Shoving the bottles into the crook of his arm, he wrestled back to his knees. Armana sidled next to him. Was she lending her back for him to prop himself up with?

"I hurt my ankle."

She nodded. Had she assumed or was it some shifter sixth sense?

His pride hated him, but the stench of burning timber motivated him to dig his fingers into her back. Strength vibrated through her. She could run another ten miles and not tire—and on this terrain.

He rose, refusing to show weakness around a creature possessing so much agility and grace. Blood rushed to his ankle. A steady throb settled into the joint, growing stronger with each flex of his muscles.

He couldn't hold back his groan as he put pressure on his foot. Oh yeah. That was a doozy of a sprain. He'd done it often enough in his days trekking off the grid that he was confident he hadn't broken anything.

Taking a step, he wobbled, using her as an aid far more than he cared to. Her heat and the softness of her fur helped keep his panic at a simmer.

She walked next to him, only advancing as he limped forward. Her steps were smooth and not jarring.

Amazing creature. And that had been his first thought after she'd crashed through his back door. And again as she'd tackled that man—shifter—whatever he was.

Had he killed the guy? A concussion would be the mildest outcome after being brained by a frying pan. Their flight had been so precipitous he hadn't stopped to think about it.

It bothered him. For all his troubles in the world, he

hadn't physically hurt anyone. He'd put Cassie's safety at risk, and he'd stymied her personal growth those months they'd spent running through the woods from his imagination. But she'd been relatively unharmed. And it'd been just her and him, and no one else had gotten caught up in his delusions.

How had he known to take Armana's side anyway? She'd broken into his house, just like the other one. Yet he would've followed her anyway and fuck all of it, whether it was a hallucination or not. That was one vision he didn't want to go away.

Despite their hobbling rate, his throat burned and his lungs tightened. The smoke in the air was getting thicker. His breathing had recovered from the mad flight through the trees and the most strenuous workout he'd had in years. His time in the gym had fortified his mind as well as his body, but the smoke was undoing all of his gains.

The wolf sneezed. He tried to pick up the pace, ignoring the stabs of pain when he put pressure on that ankle. Worse was when his foot would roll over the uneven land. His fist was twisted in her fur and he forced himself to loosen his grip.

She might not be injured, but she had to be more sensitive to the pollution than him. She didn't show it. They continued. He craned his head around, half expecting to find strange men appearing through the haze. Listening for them did no good; the crackle of the fire was growing louder.

Had the fire department been called? The roar of the blaze was too loud for him to hear sirens.

They were in the middle of nowhere and neither of them had a phone. Armana probably hadn't thought of making him carry it when she'd...stripped. She had said that the Guardians were on their way. Did that mean they patrolled this land and would know it was in trouble?

He squinted through the din ahead of him. The air

wavered, like it was flowing against an invisible obstacle. Armana's head lifted and she looked from the odd view to him.

"We're here?" he asked.

She dipped her head.

It was like a wall, an invisible force or fence line he couldn't see that blocked the flow of the smoke. How were they going to get across?

Armana stopped. He jerked forward, catching himself with his fingers twisted in her hide. Agony wicked up his leg and his calf cramped.

He sucked in a breath and wheezed it out. A coughing fit followed.

Armana remained still. Gray hacked and sputtered. If he didn't get out of this smoke soon, he'd be worthless as more dirty air filled his lungs.

Finally, he dragged in a half-clean breath and opened his eyes. A large man stood in front of him, a black rag tied across his face.

Gray was tempted to move in front of Armana, but his awkward protective instinct would only end up with him wobbling and her having to catch him anyway.

"Gray Stockwell?" the man asked in a deep, calm voice. Gray wanted to squirm under his piercing hazel stare. If the guy said he had X-ray vision, Gray wouldn't be surprised.

Gray nodded. He was used to being on the tall side for a man, but this stranger dressed in black from head to toe topped him by a few inches, and his shoulder width made Gray look scrawny in comparison.

"I'm Commander Fitzsimmons," the man said only loud enough for Gray to hear over the noise of the fire. "Can you follow me or do you need to be carried?"

The boss of the Guardians. The man in charge of Jace. Jace, who was like his mother and could turn into a wolf?

Gray mentally shook his head. He wouldn't have time to think about all of this later if he didn't get moving.

"As long as Armana can tolerate me using her as a crutch, I can walk," Gray croaked. He needed water.

Armana sneezed, followed by three more like she was trying to clear out her nostrils.

Commander Fitzsimmons's gaze flicked over them and he turned.

The closer they got to the invisible force field, the better Gray could see the other side. Where Gray was blanketed by a gritty fog, crystal clear air was only yards away.

The commander strode to the border where the land flattened and the cluster of trees thinned out. Gray didn't have to waste as much energy struggling over the ground, but it was difficult to keep up with the commander.

The man walked right through the wall. Gray stalled, but Armana turned her head and touched her nose to his knee. She knew better than to nudge his injured leg. This whole shifter business was easier to tolerate when she was saving his ass. It'd be easier to look at Jace with more than distrust— easier not to question the new reality he found himself in.

They crossed through. A brief tingling over his skin and a lungful of fresh air were the only signs that they'd made it to the other side.

Armana lifted her head. She was sucking in clean breaths. Her throat had to burn like his, but the tightness was easing to the point where he didn't feel like he was going to cough up a black lung.

Commander Fitzsimmons stopped. He must've sensed that they needed a minute to clear their heads and gather themselves. Gray assumed they were now in a safe zone, but he didn't really know. He didn't know what he knew at this point.

"West Creek's rural fire department is on the blaze,"

Commander Fitzsimmons said. How did he know? "It's eaten several hundred acres." Displeasure rippled through his features. "We're going to have to drop the wards to keep them from discovering our security."

Gray brushed the back of his forearm across his face. Dirt and dust dug into his skin. His jeans were grungy from sweat and the slide down the ridge. His shirt had small holes punched into it from rocks and roots. But he'd made it this far with only a sprained ankle and his meds.

So far so good.

The commander lifted his chin to Gray but spoke to Armana. "He's going too slow. We need to clear out before the fire department comes tromping through here."

Armana flowed into a woman. And that's what it was. He couldn't pinpoint the exact moment she went from canine to human. It didn't look painful. She made it a serene motion that took nothing more than a simple thought.

And now she was naked. He averted his gaze. Her people might not be modest, but talking to a beautiful woman with lush bare breasts and hips that invited the eye made him modest as hell.

"You take his injured side," she said to the other man.

Gray was helpless as the commander planted himself next to him and grabbed his pill bottles before throwing one of Gray's arms over his shoulder. Gray's fluster was pushed aside by a nude Armana curving herself into his other side.

His mind wanted to analyze the feel of her heat pressed into him and all the fantasies it prompted. He clamped his teeth down and stared straight ahead.

"Ready" was all he said. Time to get this over with.

They mostly carried him the rest of the way. He mimed the walking motion, but the commander was taller and used it to his advantage to lift Gray until he was at the mercy of the Guardian. Armana managed to keep his injured foot from hitting the ground.

The trees grew taller, wider, with expansive canopies that sheltered the ground. Interspersed in the landscape were tidy cabins. Some had wraparound porches. A couple had nice flower beds and even stretches of gardens. Were one of these Cassie's?

Was he going to finally see where she lived, where she'd made her home and wouldn't let him in? It only took a kidnapping attempt to get him here.

He stomped the derision down. It wasn't a healthy emotion. Dr. Sodhi would tell him that he couldn't dwell on what he couldn't control.

Didn't mean that he didn't feel like a beggar when it came to Cassie's life. Armana could do something as simple as stopping by. Had Commander Fitzsimmons been over for supper? Had drinks?

That line of thinking would do no good. Pain must be making him cranky. Cassie was the light of his life. She could do no wrong. He was the father, and he always assumed responsibility.

Gray focused on the massive log structure they were heading toward. Its peaked and arched windows blended into their surroundings by reflecting the trees and sky back on themselves. The timber used to build the lodge was natural camouflage.

The area was quiet, but he felt stares boring into him. Real or not?

"Dad!"

The others didn't stop for Cassie, but he craned his neck around. Cassie sprinted for them in a pair of jean cutoffs and a plain pink tee, her short hair bouncing with each step. It was hard to look at her as an adult and not see a ten-year-old girl baiting a fishhook.

She caught up with them and fell in step. Always his calm and collected child, she didn't pepper them with questions, nor did she ask how he was doing. Physically she could see he was okay, and they both knew that his appearance didn't indicate his mental status.

They were at the rear of the lodge. The front must be really impressive, but he wasn't here for a tour. Another wisp of resentment curled through him. He hadn't been invited here to see the place.

Cassie rushed ahead to open the door. Inside was a dim foyer that split off in different directions. The polished wood interior was just as appealing as the outside but with no adornments, no decorations, nothing that indicated what kind of people lived here. Even his psych ward had had more decorations.

They reached a room that looked a lot like a hospital suite. Two cots covered in white sheets were situated in the middle and cabinets lined the walls. The antiseptic smell shuttled him back to his time in the behavioral health ward of Freemont's hospital.

He didn't need assistance to sit on a cot, but he forced himself to appreciate the help.

"I left Jace a message an hour ago," said Cassie to Commander Fitzsimmons. "Have you heard from him yet?"

The commander shook his head. "He's with one of the twins. I tried Malcolm, but he didn't answer either."

Cassie's features pinched and she feathered a strand of hair behind her ear. Gray hated seeing his daughter distressed.

Another man came in. If Gray were to guess, he'd say they were about the same age. But then Armana claimed to be much older than she looked.

Commander Fitzsimmons didn't waste time. "It's his left ankle. Give him a quick once-over and make sure we didn't miss another injury." He turned a serious look on Cassie. The guy had bad news and he wasn't going to say anything in front of a crowd. "We'll need to talk once we get this sorted out."

Color drained from Cassie's face. Gray's protective nature reared. He planted his hands on the edge of the cot, not sure what he would do, if he could do anything.

The movement didn't escape Cassie's notice, or any of the others. Tension flowed thick through the room.

"Are you hurt anywhere else?" Cassie asked.

Gray shook his head and glanced from her to the commander. "Are you in trouble?"

"We're trying to determine what kind of trouble, but not the kind you're thinking. The safest place for me is here. These shifters are my friends...and family." Her gaze dropped, like she thought that would hurt his feelings.

Except for the trouble his mental illness had caused, he prided himself on being a good father in many ways. Cassie had found a place here, these people protected her, and that was what he wanted for her. It was his own selfish nature that wanted to make sure he was a part of her life also.

Dr. Sodhi said it wasn't selfish, but all the therapy in the world couldn't stop Gray from not wanting to cause more problems in Cassie's life.

And that's what prompted him to ignore her reaction to the commander's foreboding words. "Aside from a few scratches, it's just the sprained ankle. Pretty minor considering everything we've been through."

He met Armana's gaze. They'd had a harrowing flight through the woods. Now what? He didn't want to see her leave, but he wanted fiercely for her to get dressed. He wanted just as fiercely to hold the marvel that was her body.

She lifted a shoulder defined with gentle swells of muscle. "I've been through worse."

It wasn't said in a way to belittle the events of the day, or to address all the ways in which she claimed they were different. She just stated it as a fact.

Actually, until the fire, he'd been through worse, too.

"This is Doc," Commander Fitzsimmons said. "He'll patch you up, and Cassie and my mate will get you situated." He tipped his head and left the room. Authority oozed from the man's voice in the way he carried himself. No wonder he was in charge.

Doc opened a few drawers and Cassie planted herself in a chair by the wall.

Armana glanced around as if looking for an excuse to stay. Or was it only his imagination? "Well, I shall return to my room and get cleaned up."

"I can't thank you enough for your help, Armana," Cassie said.

"It was nice to be useful again." Her gaze flitted away and her blue eyes darkened. "Please let me know as soon as you hear from Jace." She left and Gray glued his gaze to the far wall to keep from staring at her backside.

Doc crossed over to him, his arms loaded with gauze, tape, and a damp rag. No one said anything as Doc dressed his wound. Then he rattled off a few after-care directions.

"Alex will be here shortly. She'll get you situated in one of the guest rooms. I recommend you don't go anywhere."

When Doc left, Gray slid his gaze to his daughter. She was staring pensively at the door.

Something beyond his attack and injury was bothering her. "Are you going to share what's worrying you?"

CHAPTER 5

*G*uilt simmered in Cassie's gaze. "Armana told you what she is—what the rest are?"

"I saw for myself." But he still didn't know what to believe.

"You can understand why they'd have to be so secretive. When I mated Jace, I knew what I was getting into and that someday I would have to deal with what to tell you."

Yes, his disease.

She chewed on her lip while her hands gripped her knees, her knuckles almost white. He'd never seen this level of anxiety in her. This time, it wasn't about his schizophrenia.

"What would you have to tell me?" *Or not tell me?*

"They are very strict about who knows about them, and since I won't die until Jace does, that leaves the potential for me to live for years beyond a normal human life span. I'll look like this most of that time."

Armana had made similar claims. His daughter might outlive him. But that was the way it was supposed to be.

"They have ways to combat humans knowing about them." Cassie's gaze was direct. He couldn't help the pride that swelled. She never shied away from a difficult conversation.

"What ways? Is not knowing what I'd be able to believe not enough?"

"They can tamper with memories. And I'm worried that if they do that with you, it'll have more serious repercussions than it would with someone who doesn't suffer from mental illness."

Oh. They could wipe his mind? Why did that seem outside the realm of possibility when he'd just seen Armana turn into a wolf?

But his mind wasn't normal. He sighed and scrubbed his face. The evening had worn on and although the sun stayed out past ten p.m. in the summer, it was now dark and he was tired.

"Let's not worry about that now then." Her life was startlingly full of secrecy. It was too much to think about right now.

A tall woman breezed into the room. She had vivid green eyes and a faux hawk of glossy black hair, and she carried as much authority as Commander Fitzsimmons.

She must be that man's wife—mate, or whatever they called it.

"'Sup, chickadees. I need to get you bedded down for the night." Alex's voice was as full-bodied as the rest of her, and even though Gray knew nothing about her, he preferred her over the commander, if only because Cassie's tension abated.

"Can he just stay with me? I'd feel better, since Jace isn't home yet."

Warmth infused Gray. *You want to be with Cassie for the same reason.* He needed to know she was safe, and he didn't want her home alone and scared. That wasn't usually like her, but this was an extenuating circumstance.

Alex shrugged and she looked off in the distance, her eyes

going momentarily blank. "Yeah, he said it was okay. Just don't go walking around nekkid, because the cameras will be aimed at your cabin. I know how chaste you humans get."

Gray eased himself off the cot and gingerly placed his weight on his foot. His muscles had stiffened in the short time he'd been sitting. That was one of the most bothersome signs of aging. Losing his agility motivated him to take better care of himself.

"Do we have any crutches around?" Cassie asked.

Alex went to a tall cupboard and withdrew a pair. She adjusted the length and handed them over. "Doc is nothing if not prepared. We use them sometimes if we have a wicked owie that takes more time to heal."

He used the crutches to hobble behind Cassie and Alex as they headed back out the door they had come in. Humid night air enveloped him and reminded him that he had dried sweat and caked dirt all over him and his clothing was in tatters.

The path to Cassie's cabin was fairly worn and caused little trouble with the crutches.

Cassie and Alex murmured to each other, and he couldn't make out what they were saying over his labored breathing. Was Alex reassuring her or warning her about how they were going to "deal" with him?

They reached the base of the steps going up to the porch. Alex touched a hand to Cassie's shoulder before she wandered off. As she walked past him, she said, "Get some rest. It always gets crazier before it gets calmer."

He hopped up the stairs. Cassie placed herself behind him like she was going to catch him if he fell. What an ominous warning Alex had left him with. But there was a note of support in her voice, and the more people to look after Cassie if he was gone, the better.

Cassie showed him around the little two-bedroom cabin.

Her home wasn't adorned much more than the lodge with its nature-scape wall hangings and neutral-toned furniture. The two bedrooms each had a bed and a couple of small dressers. Her and Jace's room had a quilt and another wildlife painting. She was never one to dwell on appearances. He thought back to his own home. Like father, like daughter.

The loss of his wife caught him off guard at unexpected times, like this one, and it was as if he resumed mourning where he'd left off the last time her absence was hurtfully obvious. Lillian would've dragged Cassie out shopping, laughing and chatting over what pictures would look best. They would've hit up flea markets and thrift stores. Lillian had always been good at pulling Cassie out of her own head.

"So, that's all there is here," Cassie said when they finished in the living room. "You go shower. The bed is already made, and I'll see you in the morning."

He rolled his eyes. The corner of his mouth hitched up. "I'll go shower. You get us something to drink because I know you're not going to get any sleep tonight. I'll stay up with you."

Her eyes misted over and she nodded. "Thanks, Dad."

His little girl needed him, and dammit, he was gonna be there for her.

ARMANA PACED wall to wall in her tiny room. She'd cleaned up before going to bed, but sleep had been elusive. Cassie was safe, Gray was safe, but no one had heard from Jace or Malcolm yet.

She dug deep into her well of restraint to keep herself from leaving Jace a message every five minutes and texting him every other minute to ask if he was okay.

It was early in the morning. Would Cassie and Gray be

awake yet? Armana couldn't stand herself anymore. She was going to crawl out of her skin. Running her wolf would be a good solution, but she wanted to talk to Cassie and Gray as soon as they were awake. They were both too human for her to walk in naked to chat after a shift.

Though small talk was the last thing she wanted to do. She wanted to interrogate, dismantle rooms, hell, dismantle *people* to find answers about her son.

He was good at his job, she had to have faith in that. The answer might be as simple as him being in a place with poor cell reception. Which was almost every village that shifters lived in.

She pulled her hair back into a ponytail and changed out of the tank and underwear she usually slept in. They were rumpled from her tossing and turning. She selected a pair of black pants that bordered on sweatpants and a simple yellow cotton tee. After toeing into her sandals, she stepped outside.

Judging by the morning's weather, it was going to be a beautiful day. She wouldn't enjoy one second of it until she knew Jace was safe. She couldn't even call Maggie because the commander wanted to limit the spread of worry until they knew what was going on. Armana didn't disagree, but she could've used her daughter's support.

It was unfair to expect Cassie to offer her any support. She had to be frantic in her own low-key way, but they could lean on each other. And Cassie had her father. Armana didn't have anyone.

Story of her life since that tragic night Bane died.

Her stomach clenched like it wanted to announce its hunger, but she was too upset to feel it. Instead it cramped and churned.

There were sounds of movement around her as Guardians and trainees prepared for the day. They all granted her a wide swath as usual. She'd tracked their habits, an old skill of hers she hadn't left behind in Lobo Springs. She knew the youngest trainee stargazed on nights when his past refused to quit haunting him. The twin Guardians went to the local shifter club no less than three times a week. They left together, they came back together, and they probably fucked the same females together. She knew the property, the people, and their habits. If Commander Fitzsimmons ever wanted to know if there was something hinky going on, all he had to do was hit her up. But she never offered. It wasn't her business. Not anymore. When Bane had died, she'd put her head down and concentrated on blending in.

But her isolation didn't expand her social circle. None of the Guardians and the trainees knew what to make of her and it was like they sensed the undercurrent of unease between her and Jace.

She'd set out to change that, but not much time had passed since their tenuous reconciliation. And without Cassie's encouragement, they wouldn't have made it as far as they had.

Taking one step at a time up Cassie's porch, Armana made sure that not one plank of wood squeaked. Her body was primed and ready to bolt if she sensed they had better things to do.

She knocked softly on the door and listened closely. No voices or movement carried from inside.

Had they gone to the lodge already to talk to Commander Fitzsimmons? Did Cassie have new information?

Tendrils of anger burned through her at the thought that she might have been left out. She was Jace's mother, dammit.

She blamed the anger for spurring her to test the lock. The door was unlocked and the maternal part of her wanted to chide Cassie about the oversight. But Cassie was an adult and felt safe, and Armana wasn't going to take that away from her. Jace would never forgive her.

The door swung open without a sound. She stepped inside. A quick peek to her right made her chastise herself. Cassie was curled up in a ball in the corner of the couch, asleep, and Gray dozed in a rocking chair next to her.

Dark circles rimmed Cassie's eyes. She was wearing the same clothes she'd worn yesterday. Gray looked...good. He had cleaned up and was wearing a pair of Jace's black sweats and a black T-shirt. Lines of stress and fatigue weren't as prominent while he slumbered, but she could empathize with him as a parent. He'd earned every silver strand of hair on his head through his desire to make sure Cassie was safe and unharmed since the day she'd been born.

Maybe the affinity she felt toward Gray stemmed from the fact that they were both parents. That would explain why she was so drawn to the human man when she hadn't been drawn to any man since she'd met Bane.

She stood in the entryway watching those two sleep. What now? She could dress and go for a run, but now that she was here she didn't care to leave. Her movements would've woken a normal shifter, and while Cassie's hearing had improved since her life had been combined with Jace's, she wasn't a shifter and had to be exhausted.

How late had they stayed up?

Gray's eyes opened, his sharp inhale resonating through the room. His lack of panic at seeing someone standing in the doorway earned even more respect from Armana.

"I came to see how she was doing," Armana whispered.

Gray scrubbed his face and sat forward, the soft rustle of his clothing and the scrape of the chair against the floor loud in the room. Cassie didn't twitch.

He kept his voice low, but it was more than loud enough for Armana to hear. He could've breathed the words and she would've heard them just fine. "She finally fell asleep. She needs it."

"I couldn't sleep either." Why'd she tell him that? He didn't need to be bothered with her.

Gray rose, wincing as he straightened. He reached for a crutch and left the other resting against the wall. Using the crutch to bear his weight instead of his injured leg, he stooped down to grab an empty mug and saucer. A second one sat on the end table by Cassie.

Armana moved out of the way so Gray could get to the kitchen. She grabbed Cassie's empty cup and followed.

"Is it unusual to not hear from them for long periods of time? The Guardians?" Gray set his stuff on the counter by the sink and hobbled to the fridge.

Armana shrugged even though Gray's back was to her. A shifter would've sensed the movement. After all her time in the human world, she still compared the two species. But the last few months had been like getting reintroduced to her own kind. And it rankled. As the mate to the clan leader, she'd once been a leader of sorts.

A different life. One she'd known she was leaving when she'd fled with her children.

Gray glanced at her over his shoulder. That's right, she hadn't verbally answered.

"No, it's not unusual. Neither is poor cell reception." Normal didn't matter in this situation. They were worried.

He lobbed the block of cheese onto the square table in the kitchen and grabbed a box of crackers off the counter. After tossing that onto the table, he snagged a knife from a drawer and pivoted around with the help of his crutch. He gestured to one of the chairs.

She set her dishes next to his and took a seat. "Until we hear a peep from him, we're in a holding pattern."

He held up the cheese. She shook her head.

"Have you eaten anything since we arrived?"

Her initial response was to say of course, but when she

paused to think, no, she hadn't had a bite. "I suppose I should have a chunk."

"I managed to get a few crackers into Cassie last night. With the day we had yesterday, you would only be making yourself sick by not eating." He met her gaze. His eyes were a warm shade of brown she could get lost in. "I'm assuming shifters are the same."

A ghost of a smile played over her lips. "I suppose you two had a lot to talk about."

His features tightened and he shrugged. "It was certainly enlightening." A chuckle with a hint of scorn escaped him. "I never would've imagined talking like we did and not looking over my shoulder, expecting someone to take one or both of us away."

The breath of sadness wafting through his expression shook her. Whatever had happened between him and Cassie when she was a child had left him with a deep-seated fear that he would make the same mistake and lose her forever.

Without thinking she reached over and draped her hand across his. It was the one holding the knife, but he put it down and turned his hand to clasp hers. The move startled her, the warmth of his hand soothing her, and for the first time in a long time she felt like she wasn't alone.

Their eyes met and in the depths of his she recognized the same feeling.

"I would say that I think you understand me, but I don't think your mind is messed up like mine." He released her and picked his knife back up. He started slicing the cheese, his expression sheepish.

He was hard on himself, that was obvious. She was trying to figure out what was wrong when his gaze landed on the cupboards by the fridge.

"I'll grab the plates." She jumped up and grabbed two, then a third just in case Cassie woke up. Setting only two plates on the table hinted at a level of intimacy Armana wasn't ready to think about, much less have witnessed.

"No one faults you for any level of disbelief," Armana said. "I can't imagine finding out that I was surrounded by a world so different from mine, one I knew nothing about." In addition to the other challenges he had to face.

Gray snorted. "Part of my mind is still trying to convince me not to believe it, while the other part gleefully encourages me to buy into everything. What happened yesterday? I'm already wondering if there is something wrong with me. And the sucker punch is that I can't even call my doctor and talk to him about it because I'd be putting Cassie in danger, and I know for sure that he'd recommend inpatient therapy."

Back when she'd lived among the shifters, raising her family, she'd scorned humans and their pitiful problems. She used to say that humans and their problems were like babies crying because their candy got taken away, while shifters had to deal with their troubles for eternity.

Then she'd lived among the humans but had still clung tightly to a healthy dose of hubris. She had made enough friends to really learn what happened in their lives and the repercussions of it. Her hubris had turned to humility.

"I am sorry," she said.

"There's nothing for you to be sorry for. If it weren't for you, who knows where I'd be."

He would've been wishing he were dead.

She heard Cassie stretch and stand up in the other room, but when Cassie appeared at the door, Gray's brows popped up.

"Peanut, I was hoping you could get a little more sleep in." He divided the cheese he'd sliced among all of their plates and opened the cracker box.

Cassie shuffled in and took a seat. "I'm surprised I slept as much as I did."

They didn't talk as they munched on their meager fare. Cassie stared into space, Gray glanced from his daughter to Armana, and Armana stared at her plate.

A loud chime sounded. All of their heads snapped up. Cassie gasped and jumped up, digging her phone out of her pocket.

"It's Jace." She rushed out of the room.

Armana exchanged a glance with Gray. The mom in her wanted to rush after Cassie, and she might've if Gray hadn't been here. As long as his presence helped her suffer through the weight of not knowing, then she'd consider him her anchor.

Armana and Gray sat in silence while waiting for Cassie to finish and return. She was speaking in hushed tones in the living room. Her tone vibrated with tension and Armana's apprehension rose a few notches. Cassie should sound relieved, excited.

And Cassie had been around shifters long enough to keep her voice pitched low enough for only Jace to hear.

Something was wrong.

Armana pinched the bridge of her nose and sucked in a measured breath.

"You don't think everything is okay?" Gray broke into her thoughts. She should be irritated. Decades ago, she'd literally bitten a pack member while she was in the middle of an anxiety attack. Bane had been off confronting the nasty bastard ultimately responsible for his death and she'd had small kids to care for and pack members tattling on each other to her. Anyone who had bothered her then had felt her wrath. She used to be vicious when she thought the moment called for it. Then life had become about the survival of her remaining children and she'd built a protective shell around herself.

Being with Gray offered nothing but solace. She didn't

61

bother blowing smoke to cover up her emotions.

"I can't make out her words, but no, all is not well."

"I can't imagine what you're going through. I know Cassie is in the other room and even though I still worry about her, at least she's here. And according to her, she's surrounded by people, beings—whatever—who are protecting her and everyone else here. But your son goes running into the fire."

Armana gave him a small smile. It wasn't often her kind acknowledged what parents went through. Stay proud. Stoic. It was all a badge of honor. To run around fearful and confused was an insult to their entire race.

"In many cases, he creates the fires," she said. "My daughter, too."

Gray's eyebrows rose, then he nodded. "That's right. Cassie said his sister was law enforcement in another town."

"Village, yes. That's what we call them. Villages or colonies. I… It's not like our kind to show weakness, but I've lived among humans too long. I know that expressing the occasional pang of fear or dismay doesn't break us."

"I get that."

Her forehead creased. She hadn't expected him to commiserate about suppressing feelings.

He pushed his plate away. What little appetite they'd had disappeared when the phone rang. "I have a hard time telling Cassie what's really going on in my life. If I have a bad day at work, is she going to worry that I'm on the verge of relapse? What about if I'm cranky and short of sleep? Is she going to think my meds aren't working?"

Ah yes. He had his own reason for a consistent show of strength. "It's more than that. I don't know what Cassie told you about Jace's past, but I failed him when he needed me the most."

"It might not surprise you that she didn't mention much of anything about Jace's past. When she first met him, she said he was estranged from his mom and sister. Then last year, she mentioned that Maggie had found him and was in the same line of work, and you two were talking again." The corner of his mouth hitched.

"We're talking again. Not much more than that."

Cassie appeared in the doorway. Her hand shook as she pushed her hair off her pale face. "He's, uh, he couldn't talk long. He has to report to the commander."

Armana silently cheered her boy. He should've reported in first, talked to Cassie later, but since they couldn't communicate like shifter mates could, he'd shirked duty for a few moments to speak to her.

Again, Gray surprised her with his easy manner. He didn't jump on Cassie for information but waited patiently. The girl was trying to gather herself.

"He and Malcolm raided a house where they thought girls were being stored, but it was a trap. They had to run...on foot. He couldn't tell me where he was at, but they found a phone as soon as they could. He said the commander should fill us in on the rest after Jace reports to him."

"More waiting, huh?"

Cassie rubbed her eyes. "Yeah. He's not out of the woods yet. Pun intended, but not funny. I'm going to shower."

She slogged away like the weight of the forest was on her shoulders. Armana collected their food and dishes and cleaned up. Gray wrestled to his feet and planted himself by the sink to wash. Armana fell in beside him with a dish towel for drying.

She wouldn't read more into it than was there, but it was hard not to compare Gray to her deceased mate. Bane hadn't been a domesticated male. He'd been a great father and a loving mate, but supporting his partner with all the household chores had been beneath him. He was the leader; he had no time to even clean up his spot at the table.

63

Gray scrubbed the teacups from the previous evening. "What has Cassie told you about being taken away from me?"

"Not much. I'm guessing that a lack of explanation will be a common theme."

Gray chuckled softly. The muscles in his biceps flexed as he rinsed the cup and handed it to her. Finally, she had something to do other than watch his body move out of the corner of her eye.

"You'd be right. Everything was normal. Lillian and I were diligent about my treatment, and honestly I got by treating myself with little more than a really strong dose of vitamin B." He fell quiet. "Maybe that's where we went wrong. When she fell ill, it took her so fast that I lost it."

Sickness. Her kind was spared from that form of suffering. Bane had been taken quickly, along with her oldest son. It wasn't better, but it had probably saved her sanity.

"I might've taken more precautions, sought treatment earlier," he said. The disappointment with himself was obvious as his brow drew down. How long ago had it been?

"Or you might've been so wrapped up in your grief and raising a young child that you did only what you needed to do to survive each day." That was what those dark years after Bane's and Keve's deaths had been like.

"True. The voices started before she passed. Then the hallucinations. I was standing by her casket, seeing a bunch of men in black. It was like Agent Smiths were hiding everywhere." At her quizzical look, he clarified. "It's a movie reference. *The Matrix*."

"That's right." She chuckled. "I'd forgotten about that." She'd lost herself in movies after the kids had gone to bed and she couldn't run in the woods. Once Maggie reached adulthood, she'd taken to jogging and walking, but sleepless nights had called for cable.

"Anyway, I bought a bunch of survival supplies and went

on the run." He waved his soapy hand around. "We were perma-campers, really. I made zero arrangements and the school was the one that initiated the call to law enforcement. Social services got involved and a vacationer reported seeing us..." He lifted a shoulder and she couldn't pry her gaze off the ripple of muscle. He was rather fit for a human.

"You were institutionalized?"

"They called it inpatient therapy. I couldn't get Cassie back once I got out and I didn't fight it." His brow creased. He must think he should have tried.

It was like a dark cloud hung in the kitchen when bright rays shone through the window.

Now might be a good time to share her story.

"A rogue shifter couldn't overthrow my mate so he hired vampires to attack our village. My mate and my son, Keve, died in the battle. Then the bastard came to threaten Maggie later that night." Armana wanted to spit. "The dirt hadn't even settled on their graves. I fled with Jace and Maggie. Like you, no arrangements were made."

"Solid reason, though. Not a fabrication of your mind that ruined your life."

Armana couldn't argue.

"Is he dead?" Gray asked. "The one that plotted the whole thing?"

"Yes, but it wasn't until recently. He tried to finish the job with Maggie. Her mate killed him."

"Good." The dishes were done. Gray shut the water off but didn't move.

He stared at the faucet. She waited a moment, but he didn't move.

"Gray?" She touched his arm.

He jerked, his gaze flying to her hand.

She didn't know what to say, but chose, "What I said was real. I am real."

His expression softened. "I certainly hope so." His voice dropped low. He shook his head. "I mean, not about your tragedy."

"I know." They were inches away from each other, her hand still on his forearm. His eyes focused on her lips. When was the last time a man had looked at her like that, like he needed her to be as real as the warm rays of the brilliant summer sun in the sky?

Her breath caught. She liked his reaction to her. They were more than two parents worried for their children and recovering from the mistakes they'd made in the past.

They were more than the world had made them. They were primal, raw beings who had needs.

Needs that certainly for her hadn't been met in countless blue moons.

Desire and pure male interest rolled off of Gray and sweet Mother Earth, it was intoxicating. Her lips parted as his gaze filled with heat. She swayed closer and his head dipped.

Her sensitive ears picked up a door shutting and footsteps heading their way.

Armana blinked and stepped back. The spell that was Gray's attraction was broken.

Cassie rounded into the room. "Do you guys think we should just wait or head to the lodge and bug the commander?"

Cassie stopped, her gaze jumping between her and Gray. Armana's heart pounded. Cassie didn't know, she couldn't. Her human senses couldn't smell the spike of desire in the room.

Gray spun around and leaned against the sink. He cleared his throat and pushed off to frown behind him. A wet spot lined the back of his admirable ass.

Armana's giggle couldn't be stopped. She slapped her

hand in front of her mouth. When was the last time she'd giggled of all things?

Cassie's brow furrowed as she looked between them, then her gaze dropped to where Gray was scowling at his backside. Her lips twitched, and she sputtered into a chuckle.

Gray started laughing with them. It was good for all of them. They'd been riding on a wave of anxiety. Mostly it was a good distraction from the thought that Gray had been about to kiss her. Or had she been about to kiss him? The energy crackling between them was mutual.

Armana's humor died, but the lightness remained. "The commander will be focused on the mission. We might need to go to the lodge to get answers."

There was a knock on the door. Cassie darted to answer it. Armana smelled Commander Fitzsimmons before he stepped into the kitchen. The cabins weren't large and there were already three of them hanging out in one room. He didn't have to squeeze in, but his fierce presence overflowed the space. Dressed in black tactical clothing, he cast shadows in all directions.

"Jace talked to you." He spoke to Cassie.

She nodded hesitantly, as if afraid Jace would get in trouble for calling her first. But there was no flash of irritation or promise of retaliation in the male. He was mated himself and perhaps understood how the mind worked when it came to putting love before duty.

Bane wouldn't have tolerated that lapse in protocol. He had been a stickler for rules and honor and all the rest of the bullshit that came with leadership. Armana had, too. At one time.

The commander glanced at the empty seats at the table. He almost looked like he was going to sit but then decided not to linger. "The shifters they're after are more organized than we gave them credit for. They're trolling all over the region, kidnapping humans to sell as blood slaves to the vampires." A muscle flexed in his jaw. "And shifter children to sell overseas to the highest bidder."

Armana blinked and Cassie gasped. Overseas? Their kind and vampires didn't often move away from areas where they'd been settled for centuries. If they did, they went to other places where shifters had lived for centuries and mated into those packs. They didn't migrate as a whole. To go so far beyond their own borders to victimize their own kind was unheard of.

But modern times made it harder to keep their presence from being detected with the use of smart phones and instant access to video. It also made it harder to contain the damage that rogue shifters could cause.

"They expected to get caught and were prepared for it," the commander continued. "Jace and Malcolm are going to reorient and keep going after them. Bennett and Harrison, Malcolm's twin, are on their way with extra supplies. We're going to nail these rogues."

Cassie nodded, her relief plain now that the commander was sending a couple of his best, who happened to be two shifters without loved ones who could be targeted. Bennett had a mate, but she was safely ensconced in her cabin and worked around the lodge. Armana knew her well enough to know that anyone attacking Bennett's mate was in for a nasty surprise.

"That brings us to you." The commander's stare bored into Gray. To the human's credit, he didn't shrink under the formidable gaze that made cocky new recruits squirm. "You need to stay here with Cassie until this blows over. And... I'll go to the Synod and plead your case, but I can't promise anything. They'll likely rule to take your memories."

Cassie shook her head. "But—"

The commander cut her off with a look that said he

understood her argument perfectly but the decision was out of his hands. "His condition. I get it. They get it. But it's a slippery slope. Where do we stop allowing humans to know of our presence?"

Cassie's lips pursed. "There are also his appointments and medication."

"I have a week's supply left," Gray said.

Armana wanted to growl with frustration, both for the fact that Gray couldn't be given the gift of knowing about his daughter's life and because a week's supply wasn't enough. The rogue shifters had broken ties with a pack by disobeying laws and not sticking around for the consequences. They were on the run and crafty. It could take a month or more to track all involved down, even with four of the best Guardians on their trail.

Cassie shook her head. "You shouldn't miss your appointments, either, Dad. It's my professional opinion that it's more critical than ever to not lapse in your treatment." Her gaze flicked to the commander and darkened. "Especially if they think they're going to tamper with your mind."

Cassie's tone sounded like she was going to have a "chat" with whoever was in charge, but it wouldn't change the final decision. The protection of their kind versus a human's brain? Armana knew what they'd choose. And from the commander's regretful look, so did he. She didn't envy him. He carried out the Synod's orders and often his own wishes and opinions had to take a backseat.

She'd been the mate of a colony leader. She knew the toll it took, carrying out a higher power's commands, in addition to the personal cost of disciplining those who were too selfish to see past their own desires. That type of conflict had led to Bane's and Keve's deaths.

The little she knew of Gray she liked and respected, and yes, she'd grudgingly admit she was attracted to him. But

69

she'd stand behind the Synod's decision lest any dissension filter down to her kids and Cassie.

Commander Fitzsimmons's gaze bored into her like he could hear her thoughts. To him, she was the wild card. Cassie's wishes were obvious and Gray was going to do what was best for his daughter.

She inclined her head. Understanding infused his gaze. Her acceptance of the situation made her an ally in handling Cassie. The girl's emotions and feelings for her dad were going to cloud her decisions, and if the commander thought Armana would ply Cassie with treasonous ideas, he'd put a stop to it.

No, she wasn't going to do that. She'd help Cassie, support her, buffer the girl's reactions so they didn't interfere with Jace's work, but she wouldn't work against the government and possibly cost her son his job.

The commander finally spoke. "I'll allow it, but we'll have to plan accordingly. They've been following him and they'll likely keep monitoring places he frequents."

"I can accompany him," Armana offered. It would help Cassie, give her peace of mind. There was no other reason for volunteering, despite the dark cloud hanging over her head that all memories of her would be taken when the Synod ruled. "Since Cassie won't be able to go to town."

The commander leveled his stare on her. How had Gray managed not to fidget under that intensity? Commander Fitzsimmons was disconcerting and she was nearly as old as him. But she'd never had to wear the mantle of responsibility he did.

"I'll send another Guardian with him," the commander said. "As Jace's mother, you are in danger."

Some days she wondered if Jace would stress over her beyond his inherent honor to do so. Maggie was another story, but the rogue would have trouble identifying Armana.

"I doubt whoever is behind the trafficking has found a thing out about me that isn't outdated. It'd give Cassie peace of mind and keep an extra Guardian free to hunt for the rogues."

The commander's sigh was barely detectable. Going rogue was the first step to becoming feral. The lack of ties to a pack and governing authority brought out the worst in their beasts. They were bred for pack living and mating for life. If these rogues were also unmated, they might spiral faster, and then the commander would have a larger problem that could explode in shifterkind's face. Feral shifters didn't care who they hurt and killed or who saw.

"Fine," he said and looked at Gray. "When's your next appointment?"

Gray's lips flattened. She didn't sense he was angry with any of them, but with himself. "This afternoon. I haven't had a chance to cancel."

"Can you reschedule?" the commander asked.

Cassie answered. "Their patient load is so heavy and scheduled out so far that I doubt they'd have an opening even before his next monthly appointment."

"Biweekly," Gray said quietly and dropped his gaze. "Since you've been married—mated—we've upped the frequency."

Cassie's jaw dropped and guilt reflected in her eyes.

Gray shrugged. "I felt like you were hiding something and I was...alone. Dr. Sodhi recommended that we meet more often."

Cassie squeezed her eyes shut and Armana didn't need telepathy to know what she was thinking. If he required more care when he genuinely hadn't known what his daughter was hiding, what was going to happen when his mind was tampered with and his memories stolen?

* * *

GRAY WANTED to kick back in the cabin all day. Play some cards with Cassie and eat cheese and crackers until he got sick of sweeping crumbs up.

Instead, Cassie had brought him some of Jace's clothing, and he was picking through it to find something that fit so he could see his shrink.

The commander was making special concessions for him and Gray didn't care what Armana said, she was putting herself in danger.

The only thing that made him feel better was that they could fill his meds and not have to worry about that for another month. He could cancel his next session with Dr. Sodhi. After all, he didn't feel like Cassie was hiding anything from him anymore and he certainly wasn't alone.

Losing his memories. He paused and stared at the pair of jeans in his hands. He'd go back to feeling like Cassie was keeping secrets. He'd have that sense of being coddled because she might be worrying that he couldn't handle the information. He'd...lose Armana.

His vision blurred and he went back to that moment at the sink. He'd almost kissed her. He hadn't kissed anyone for...a while.

After treatment and once Cassie was an adult, he'd dabbled in the dating pool. The whole effort had felt useless but he'd been a man in his prime and wanting some adult company. None of the dates had progressed beyond a few kisses or, in a couple of circumstances, casual sex. But when the relationship deepened to the point of having to share his past—and his present reality—he'd bailed in an *it's not you it's me* way.

The last several years, he'd just given up. The few times Cassie and Jace came to visit, he'd witnessed true love. Dating hadn't been appealing. Couldn't he just go straight to that without the warning talk? *Here's what you're getting if you keep seeing me...*

He focused back on getting dressed. His appointment was in an hour. Armana was picking up a new car from the lodge and he had to meet her in fifteen minutes.

Frowning at the pants, he tossed them back on the bed and chose another pair. Jace had a certain look and it was the opposite of Gray's tidy blend-into-the-crowd style. Jace rode a motorcycle and dressed accordingly. Finally, Gray found a pair that wasn't shredded at the knees and wouldn't look absurd with the athletic shoes he'd cleaned up from his flight through the woods.

He tugged them on, careful of his ankle. At least Jace had a large selection of plain tees and they weren't as baggy on Gray as he'd feared. He didn't have the bulked-up physique of his son-in-law, or whatever they call mate-in-laws, but he kept himself in shape.

Stopping to glance in the mirror before he left, he assured himself that while his hair was short, it could still get mussed. He wasn't trying to impress Armana. He was too old for that.

His body disagreed. Since she'd left to go back to her room in the cabin and rest before they went to town, his body had roared to life like he'd regressed to his early twenties. Cassie had lain down to nap after the commander had left, and Gray had gone to the guest room to do the same— only to be kept awake with images of Armana and an erection so hard he hadn't gotten a wink of sleep.

All afternoon, he'd reminded himself that he was a fifty-year-old man. Men his age did not get aroused at a moment's notice. Not that he knew many men his age. And he certainly wasn't going to tell Dr. Sodhi about his latest mental crisis.

He left the cabin and started the trek to the front of the

lodge where Armana had said she'd be waiting. What was he going to talk to Dr. Sodhi about?

He couldn't tell the doc that he hadn't imagined a thing, that Cassie had been lying. Nor could he evade the truth, that he'd really been followed. Either way, the doctor would think he was slipping away from reality.

He thought back to his last few sessions and what they'd talked about. He could still express worry for Cassie's way of life. And the worry that he was being followed still rang true. Same old, same old, really.

He rounded the lodge. Armana stood by two cars. Both were dark gray. She was talking to a young man who was almost as large as the commander. The kid was dressed like them, in jeans and a T-shirt. The obvious difference between him and Gray, other than age—and according to what he'd learned, who knew if the guy was a century older than him—was that the shifter oozed danger. He didn't look armed, but he also didn't look like he needed to be armed.

Armana looked younger than ever in jean shorts that framed long, lean legs and a fitted shirt in a dark blue that made her eyes even more vibrant.

The male turned without even acknowledging Gray's arrival. All of these people seemed to know what was around long before anything came into sight. Cassie had said their senses were heightened, and even though hers were too since she'd been mated, hers couldn't rival the sensitivity of theirs.

"We need to get you a weapon." The male scowled at Gray's shoes. "Maybe we can strap a knife to each leg without it being detected when you sit down."

Gray drifted to a stop. He had to go to his psych appointment armed? Did they have a clue what would happen if someone saw?

Armana must've read the apprehension in his face. "Gray,

this is one of the new Guardians, Declan. He's new to the area, but he's worked with Jace a few times."

In other words, she trusted him.

"I'm going follow you two and wait outside the clinic and pharmacy." He was as curt as Commander Fitzsimmons. It must be a Guardian thing. Jace gave that impression, too, except for when he looked at Cassie.

Declan went to one of the cars. He came back carrying two knives sheathed in leather holsters. "Anchor those where no one will see."

Gray accepted the weapons and weighed the steel in his hands. He'd carried bowie knives on him years ago when he'd been in bad mental shape, but these felt...saner. "I appreciate it. Thank you."

The shifter's brows popped. Had he not been expecting Gray to say something as simple as thank you?

Declan nodded and walked toward the garage. Stalked was more like it. Armana watched him walk away.

She met Gray's gaze, her eyes full of amusement. "It's times like these I feel really old. He's so young and full of attitude, but all I see is a kid in adult's clothing."

Gray chuckled. "Is he young in your world, but still older than me?"

She smiled, her bright eyes going radiant. "He's younger than Cassie. A true pup—to me anyway."

Gray kept his smile in place. In his world, calling someone a pup would be weird, but in hers maybe it was natural.

She went around the car and got in the driver's seat. He crawled into the passenger side. The car was ash gray and nondescript. He expected a sense of déjà vu, but since they weren't running for their lives this time, the trip turned into nothing more than a drive into town.

Declan remained behind them. When they drove through

West Creek and over the bridge into Freemont, Gray feared they'd lost him, but then he caught a glimpse of the car.

Armana parked outside of the hospital on the side of the behavioral health clinic. He wished it were more of a one-level building like where Cassie worked. He'd have to check in and go up several floors. If there was trouble, he'd have all those floors to go back down and escape.

"We'll wait until Declan gives me the all clear."

He relaxed in his seat. She didn't have her phone in her hand. Oh. Telepathy.

He was sitting in a car outside of a psychiatric clinic with a lady he was fiercely attracted to. She turned into a wolf and was mentally talking to another guy who could turn into a wolf.

This was going to go well.

"What's the range on your telepathy?" It sounded like a stupid question to his ears.

"It depends," she answered easily. "I don't know Declan well, so we need to be close. Within a block or so? Mates can communicate farther, and the Guardians who have been together for decades can maintain an impressive connection. But there's no definitive answer."

He nodded because what would he reply to that?

"Bane and I could communicate over a mile. He'd always let me know when he was getting close to home if he was out for a run or hunting ferals."

"How long were you two..." Together? Mated? He was learning that married was the wrong term.

Her sad smile burrowed into his soul to find a matching sense of loss. "We almost hit our century mark. We know our mates when we meet, right?" No, he hadn't known. Cassie always said that Jace had known she was the one for him, but Gray had assumed it was romantic bluster, not reality. "I wasn't young, but I wasn't ready to settle down and oh boy, neither was he. But we couldn't stay away from each other," she said wistfully.

"I knew when I saw Lillian that I wanted to marry her."

Armana's smile was genuine. "Funny how love works."

"Yeah. We were in college. She wanted to wait to get married, but Cassie came along earlier than planned." He'd never finished school, a regret that had followed him as an adult when he'd tried to find gainful employment with benefits. No technical training and no degree limited his options.

"We mated before he took leadership. It's best not to have those sorts of distractions when you're ruling a bunch of hormonal shifters who think they're alphas."

"Are all of those positions that dangerous?"

"They used to be, but it's getting better. I hope so. Maggie's mate is the leader of my old colony. He's a good kid."

They were alike in that everyone under forty was a kid.

Her eyes unfocused for a heartbeat. "Declan says it's clear."

They got out and Armana walked next to him all the way to the clinic. She hung back while he checked in, and she sat next to him in the waiting room.

This woman—shifter—Armana knew his past and his present and she was here next to him while he was going to his shrink. He hadn't ever revealed to a date that he suffered from a mental disorder and here Armana was. She knew everything.

Even if she was interested, they couldn't so much as date. Not only would it betray Cassie and Jace for him to attempt something with Armana, but he was going to lose all memory of her eventually. And he could easily fall hard for the strong, sensible woman. Losing that might drive him over the edge again.

CHAPTER 6

*A*rmana checked her watch. Gray's hour was nearly up. He hadn't seemed nervous going into the room, but he'd have to lie about details he now knew weren't paranoia.

It was so easy being around him. She hadn't had that level of comfort with Bane until years into their mating. They'd been too young and full of aggression and instinct. They'd mellowed after Keve had come along, and Bane had dived into the role of father figure.

What had Gray been like? She could picture him as a college kid doting on a young girl. Rocking a little baby.

Her mouth twitched. Bane had never been the nurturing type. When she needed a break, he'd play swords with the kids, run them through the woods. They'd sleep like the dead when she returned.

Her smile died as she heard men's voices behind a closed door. Gray and Dr. Sodhi. The doctor had given her a speculative look when he'd come out to get Gray.

She gave Gray a once-over as he emerged from the doorway. His shoulders were relaxed and he was smiling as he said goodbye to Dr. Sodhi.

They walked down to the car. She mentally cleared it with Declan first. The pharmacy was the next stop and she passed her route along to the young shifter.

Once they were inside with the doors shut, she asked, "How did the appointment go?" She was prying, but she couldn't help herself.

"Really well. I tried to act normal." His lips curved. "Well, my normal. He asked about you and I said I finally made a friend."

A warm glow started in her belly from the way he said "friend." She doubted he'd speak about a male like that.

They fell into a comfortable silence on the way to the pharmacy. She'd go inside with him there, too.

Like at the clinic, she parked and waited for Declan's all clear. He was parked in a restaurant's lot next to the CVS.

As Gray paid for his prescription, she browsed. He joined her when he was done. She was combing through their discount bin of DVDs. She had a beater DVD player that she liked binge-watching series on. The lodge had admirable technical capabilities, but she couldn't contribute money to pay for the use of it so she stayed with disks.

"Hey, *The Matrix*." He braced himself on a crutch to free a hand and snatched it up. "I don't think it's so unique anymore," he said wryly.

She chuckled and froze when Declan's voice invaded her thoughts. *There's an exit in the back of the store. Go out there and I'll swing by and pick you up.*

Gray noticed her tension and dropped the DVD back into the bin.

"We need to go out the back," she said.

He scanned the store. She'd already located all the exits

within seconds of being in the store. A byproduct of living in fear for decades.

She grabbed his arm and tipped her head close to him like they were in conversation. He automatically followed suit, thinking she was going to tell him something.

They strode down a hallway and past the public restrooms. When they reached the exit door, she stayed him with a hand. It wasn't rigged with a fire alarm, but it was a door used by employees. Perfect. They could leave discreetly.

She pushed it open and scented outside before stepping out. All sorts of smells assaulted her, from trash to exhaust fumes to greasy burgers from the eating places close by. But no other shifters.

An engine approached. That must be Declan having seen the door open.

She pulled Gray with her. He maneuvered through the exit, his bag of meds banging against his crutches. Declan approached, but a scratching sound caught her attention and the hair on the back of her neck rose.

Gray looked up the same time she did. A shadow launched from the roof onto them. She shoved Gray away and kicked out as soon as the female landed. Her foot connected with the side of the shifter's hard head.

The female grunted and fell back, which brought her closer to Gray. He stared at her like he couldn't comprehend that anyone could survive a leap from the roof—and a female, no less.

Armana lunged for the female, her fist swinging. Footsteps pounded toward them from the opposite direction that Declan was approaching from. He couldn't speed toward them. If he hit Gray, it'd be all over. The rogues could take her, but she'd be more trouble than she was worth.

Her first swing hit the female's chin. The rogue bared her

fangs and she let a right hook fly. Armana blocked it, but hands dug into her shoulders and yanked her backward.

"Get the guy," a male snarled.

Armana twisted and elbowed a midsection made of steel. He spun her with one hand and hugged her to him hard enough to suffocate her.

Declan jumped out and raced between the female and Gray. The female launched herself at Declan. Gray plastered himself to the wall, but his expression wasn't one of paralyzed fear. He set his crutches against the wall and the bag of meds dropped to the ground.

The male behind Armana wrapped his arm around her neck like a vise. His punishing grip didn't ease. She gasped for air, dug her fingers into his arms until they were slick with blood, and pummeled his knees and shins with her feet.

She was about to blackout when Gray stooped down. He disappeared from her sight and a moment later, he spun around Declan, a knife in each hand. The female shifter couldn't chase him or Declan would take her down.

Armana thought Gray was going to run past them, his face contorted with the pain of running on his ankle, but as he passed, he whipped his arm out to the side and rammed one blade into the female's beefy shoulder. She cried out, the distraction enough for Declan to tackle her to the ground and slam her head against the pavement.

Gray kept moving. The shifter holding her spun and turned, keeping her between Gray and his other knife.

Gray caught her eyes. He was planning something. His moves weren't as fast as a shifter's, but he tossed the knife and caught the blade and held it out. She snatched the handle and stabbed the blade into the thigh of the male.

He grunted, his hold loosening enough for her to drag in a breath. Armana yanked and twisted the blade until the shifter couldn't bear weight on that leg. He let her go but punched her in the kidney. She dropped.

Gray was about to lunge when the unmistakable sound of a gun with a silencer went off. Armana looked up. Red bloomed on the male shifter's forehead. She switched her gaze to Gray's shocked face. They both looked at Declan.

He grimly shot the female next.

"Silver-laced bullets," Declan said, scanning the alley to check for witnesses. "They're done for, and I've got a mess to clean up."

His gaze rose to the corner of the pharmacy building, where a security camera was mounted. He swore.

"I'll get Gray out of here; you do damage control." She ran to grab the crutches for Gray, who hadn't taken his eyes off the female he'd stabbed.

Declan scratched the back of his neck. He was young. Fighting he understood. Making the decision to let her go with the man he was supposed to protect went against his need to follow commands.

"Protecting the secrets of our people takes priority," she said. "You go in and deal with the camera and we'll clear out of here with the bodies."

Sirens blared in the distance.

With a growl, Declan popped the trunk of his car.

They loaded the two shifters up. Gray jumped in, but the apprehension radiating off him worried her.

Armana hopped into the driver's seat. "I need to get Gray out of here. You erase the footage."

Declan nodded. "Call it in for me. Tell them I need help persuading cops not to investigate."

"Will do." Armana nudged Gray to the passenger side and tossed the keys to her car at Declan.

She and Gray clambered into the car. She pulled away,

turning in the opposite direction of the sirens. Keeping her speed down, she handed her phone to Gray.

He didn't ask why but pulled up her contacts and called the commander. He calmly explained what was going on, but his eyes were a little too wide and in danger of going vacant.

Had he never stabbed anyone before? Was his mind unraveling?

He hung up the phone and set it in the cupholder.

She felt like she had to say something. "If Jace were around, this situation would be a minor nuisance."

"Why's that?" he asked woodenly.

"He's…gifted with an extra dose of…" Maybe that topic hadn't been the best idea. Explaining Jace's special abilities might be the straw on the camel's back.

Gray folded his hands in his lap. "I just stabbed a woman, there are two bodies in the trunk, and we're running from the cops. Are you afraid to say something because I can't handle it?"

"Yes." She meandered through Freemont. If she could make her way, twisting and turning, over a different bridge into West Creek, then they might be able to lose any other tails. "Some of us have special abilities beyond our heightened senses. They aren't always practical, like being able to recognize and name all the constellations. Once upon a time, that skill might've made sense."

"But Jace's?" Gray sounded impatient as he aimed his stony stare out the window.

"He can influence what people think."

Gray didn't reply. "Will he be the one stealing my memories?"

"No, they have others who can do that."

"Has Jace used his ability on Cassie?"

Her motherly instinct was to stand up for her son. "Do you think he'd do that? Or that Cassie would tolerate it?"

Gray swiveled his stare to her. "Would she know? We're only human."

"Gray, I know today has been—"

The phone rang.

He sighed and picked it up, muttering, "It's Fitzsimmons."

None of them called him just "Fitzsimmons." Gray must be reaching the peak of his give-a-shit levels.

She strained to hear what the commander was saying. Catching bits of it didn't help. Because it sounded like more strange shifters had been spotted in West Creek and they couldn't bring the bodies back to burn.

"By the river's headwaters?" Gray asked. "That's a hundred miles away."

Armana checked the gas gauge. They could make it there, but she couldn't putter around Freemont any more than she had to. She adjusted her course to take her out of Freemont.

"Fine." Gray's voice was as tight as his body language. "Nope. I'm sure Armana can hold my hand through it." He hung up the phone, and she doubted the commander was done talking.

"Gray—"

"I assume you heard all that? You said you had heightened senses and I got the impression that he was raising his voice for you."

She wished she could study him, but she had to concentrate on driving. "What's wrong?"

"We can't go back. We have bodies to dump. *Bodies*. And I don't know if I want to go back and face my daughter with blood on my hands."

She shrugged. "Jace does every day after work."

Gray whipped his head toward her.

"What? She's not a wilting flower. Your daughter is strong. Obviously, or she wouldn't be the mate of a shifter.

And deep down, you know that. You knew her strength before she mated. So what's really wrong?"

He blew out a breath and slumped in his seat. "When I was gallivanting through the woods, running from imaginary bad guys, I never hurt anyone other than myself. Cassie barely even skinned a knee. I stabbed somebody today. I would've stabbed a second person if I could've gotten to him."

He was thinking like a human. Because he was one.

"Would it help to reassure you they were really bad shifters? I doubt we're the first innocent people they've tried to hurt." She shot him a pointed look. "Or killed."

His brow dropped like he was still having trouble reconciling his actions.

"Shifters can't die from being stabbed."

His expression was suffused with disbelief.

They were nearing the edge of Freemont. When she hit the highway, she pushed the speed just enough to not get pulled over.

"Beheading, organ removal, major traumas like that will end us," she explained. "And like Declan said, silver. Yeah, we can bleed out, and if we stay like that, unable to heal, eventually we die. The little prick you gave that female? She would've healed in a couple of hours."

"That...oddly makes me feel better. But then she could've been healed enough to go after you again, or Cassie."

"Nailed it. Now do you feel better?"

"No, but I understand."

His honesty... It was becoming one of his most appealing traits, and he had so many.

"Are you hurt? That man was suffocating you, wasn't he?"

Her throat was sore, and she probably had a few fading bruises under her clothing. "I'm fine."

They rode in silence the rest of the way to the headwaters

of the river that cut between West Creek and Freemont. She stopped outside of a campground and called Commander Fitzsimmons.

"We're here," she said when he answered.

"Ditch the car. I'll have a crew swing by and grab it. I'm going to text you some coordinates. There's a safe house a mile from your position." She wasn't surprised he knew exactly where they were. "After my crew is done with disposal, they'll come get you and get you back safely."

Relief washed away her worry. Good. She didn't relish another flight through the woods when Gray was already injured. They could take it slow.

She hung up and relayed the instructions.

"Good. I'll be glad to be done with this car." Gray got out and hopped around on one foot. He withdrew his crutches and shut the door.

She'd almost forgotten the dead bodies in the trunk but he hadn't.

He went a few steps and stopped to glare at the back of the car. Then he looked around, his gaze suspicious.

She did the same. All she heard were vehicles that were still miles away, and she scented only the lingering smells of campers who'd passed through. Nothing she saw or heard could be detected by Gray.

He shook his head and hobbled off. "Which way are we going? I've gotta get away from the... I just... My mind is starting to mess with me."

"Are you hearing things?"

He nodded, his gaze pinned to the gravel. "Yes. If I can remove myself from the situation, it's best."

She glanced at the directions the commander had sent. "Through the trees. We follow a wildlife path straight to it. No regular campers should be close."

Collecting the phone and the bag of medicine, she locked

the car with the keys inside and followed him. She expected the mile to take forever, but Gray used the crutches like a walking stick, his muscular body powering him over the path. The wildlife trail was well traveled—probably by shifters.

The Guardians' resources were a marvel. They had to travel between colonies, and hotels weren't always possible. Neither was sleeping out in the elements in the middle of winter. A few scattered cabins were low-maintenance enough to provide shelter when needed.

"He said there would be canned goods for us."

"Good," Gray snapped.

Okay. His mood had darkened, not improved.

He stopped and glared over his shoulder, but not at her.

Oh hell. He wasn't having a mental breakdown, was he? "Gray, is it…?"

"Yes. I swear I hear them taunting me."

"Who?'

"Them." He turned and kept hobbling along the trail.

Stabbing someone was hard for him to reconcile. The man breaking down a door to his house was one thing, so was the frying pan Gray had used to bash him over the head.

A knife made everything too real. Or for Gray, too surreal.

"What do they say?"

He sighed and stopped. "They're telling me I'm in trouble and not to trust anybody, which is hard because they're not wrong."

No, they weren't. It hit her how hard it was for him. He'd been in a fight for his life, and his intuition had blended with the voices to tell him he was in trouble. For a man who'd had to learn how to navigate daily life based on whether he believed the voices or not, his black and white had turned all…gray.

"Oh, Gray." She closed the distance between them and stroked his face.

He flinched and paled. "My meds."

She held up the bag and his shoulders sagged.

They faced each other for a moment before he said, "The worst is what they say about you."

"The voices?" How bad was it? If he had a hard time trusting her because of them, then their stay in the cabin could turn ugly. He might try to escape and hurt himself. Worse yet, she'd have to stop him and then he'd really have a hard time around her.

"What do they say, Gray?"

His eyes glimmered with the torture he hid from everyone. "They say I'm hindering you. That you can't wait to get away from me and if anything goes wrong, it's my fault. That...once we get back, you can't wait to laugh with your friends about me."

She skimmed her thumbs along his jaw. She should stop touching him. "I can assure you that last part's not true. I don't have any friends." His expression lightened, but her humor wasn't enough to chase his demons away. "Just keep talking to me. Okay?"

He nodded. They continued along the trail.

The tidy cabin came into view. There was no porch for viewing the sunset over the trees, and it wouldn't have done any good. This far away from the lake, the trees stretched high and the landscape rolled and swooped in gentle hills.

The landing barely had space for a person, which made sense from a security standpoint. Fading wood lent the cabin a dilapidated appearance, but as they approached, the sturdiness of the structure was more apparent and the washed-out color was actually a stain. Crafty shifters. No camper would care to look around or squat here, and if they did, they wouldn't find anything useful except, hopefully, bottled water and canned goods.

"Is there anything I can do?" she asked.

Gray contemplated her offer, but the faint trace of suspicion in his eyes left her uneasy. "No. I need a quiet place to rest. I jolted my ankle pretty bad and it's been hanging down instead of being elevated. It just might be the pain making the voices louder than normal."

"Is the paranoia constant?"

"Not always," he said grimly. "It comes in phases. I'm usually militant with self-care, but the last couple of days have upended me."

And the sleepless nights, injuries, and stress were getting to him.

"Should I message the commander and tell him to give us an extra day here?"

Gray paused. "Do you think he'd go for it?"

"If I explain the situation, maybe." Probably not, but she'd try. "Let me go inside first." When Gray gave her the side-eye, she explained, "Just in case there's someone trying to claim it as their own, furry or two-legged."

He nodded. Had her words made his paranoia better or worse? She'd work on being more transparent.

The door swung open easily. No locks. That shouldn't be an issue. On the inside, there were deadbolts and latches. Perfect. She sniffed and let her senses roam. Nothing that she wouldn't expect in a cabin in the middle of the woods prickled her senses. No artwork, no frills, no decorations.

She held the door wide open. "Come in. There's a few chairs. I'll scoot two close so you can prop your foot up."

He hobbled inside and peered around. "Their decorator should be fired."

His dry tone coaxed a smile from her. "Yes. Appalling."

Moving two folding chairs together, she arranged them

MARIE JOHNSTON

so he could recline. Plush comfort wasn't available, but perhaps there was a bed or a cot he could relax in. He sat down with a heavy breath and stretched his foot onto the other chair.

His eyes drifted shut and the lines of fatigue were more apparent than she'd ever seen. Before, he'd looked strapping for a fifty-year-old human, but today, he looked his age.

There was no spare room and no bathroom beyond the great outdoors, but there were two cots folded in the corner and a trunk she hoped contained a blanket or two. The space that was supposed to be a kitchen was just a bare corner with a few boxes stacked.

Digging into them revealed canned chicken, green beans and peas, and another two boxes with bottled water.

"The good news is there's food. The bad news is there's no plumbing."

He didn't open his eyes. "Perfect."

"I'll get us something to eat and then set up the cots in the other room. I can sleep out here and keep watch and patrol occasionally while you get some rest."

He lifted his head and pinned her with his intense gaze. "I can help, too."

"I know, but you're better off resting. We still have to walk out of here tomorrow."

He frowned. "I feel useless."

"You're not." She went over to him and perched on the crate. "You and I, we're partners. If I were injured, you'd do the same thing."

"You've had the same flight through the woods, jumped down the same ravine, gotten just as little sleep, fought two shifters—no, three, counting the one in my house. You've done all the driving, and you made the same trek up here." His gaze brushed her face in a way that called up her feminine pride. "And you do it while looking better and better.

90

Your gorgeous eyes are bright, your cheeks are flushed, and your body moves like it was made for this life. Which I guess it was."

His compliments and admiration had no business making her glow like they did. It didn't help that she knew him well enough to know he was being sincere. And if she hadn't known him, she could still sense it. Honesty, respect, and male interest radiated from him. It was a potent combination.

How much had changed since she was younger and unmated? Then, only the brawny, quick-tempered males who picked fights with anyone and everyone had garnered her attention. When she'd first spotted Bane, he'd just won such a fight. He'd only been traveling through her village and had challenged their leader. Bane had been bloodied, battered, and pulsing with more energy to expend.

She'd expended it all right. All night long.

She could imagine how Gray had met his late wife. Long looks across a classroom or a crowded campus. Nervous chatter, summoning the courage to ask her out. Late dinners rolling into lingering kisses until they'd finally slept together. Awkward, sweet first times.

Fifty years ago, she would've looked down on that with utter derision. How...tame.

Suddenly, tame sounded nice. She'd had enough violence in her life. Most shifters accepted it, but she'd lived among humans too long. The majority lived a peaceful life, working hard to maintain a safe and serene environment, in their home at a minimum, if they couldn't influence the world outside their doors.

They were standing in silence. He gazed at her, not quite a stare, but as if he wondered what she'd do about his words. It was going to get horribly awkward if she didn't move.

"You're right. I was born for this kind of life, but it doesn't mean I wish for it. Not anymore." His look grew questioning, but she didn't elaborate.

She crossed to the food crates and dug out beans and chicken. There were no plates or utensils other than a can opener.

"It's going to be finger food tonight," she said and gathered the supplies. She handed Gray a couple bottles of water and went outside to open and drain the cans.

Back inside, she pulled a chair closer to him. They ate, nimbly digging and picking scraps of food.

Gray sat forward, his leg still propped. "I've had worse."

She smiled. "Me, too. Slugs to be specific. My wolf prefers red meat like I do."

He dug into the bag of medicine and withdrew the bottle. After washing down the pill, he went back to eating. "Are you separate entities?"

"No. We talk about our wolves like they're separate, but they're not. I think the same when I'm in my other form. But it's like there's a part of my brain that processes the world through a wolf's eyes."

Gray deftly grabbed the last of his green beans and looked at her like he was waiting for her to continue.

"As a wolf, I'm a hunter. I'm part of nature. I can't talk so I process thoughts into actions. When I say she prefers red meat, I'm talking about the dismay I feel when I gaze at a slimy, wiggly thing when my belly is grumbling for real food. I can't say 'I'd rather have a steak' but I know I'd rather have a steak."

"Makes sense. I wish I were as comfortable with the other part of me. If it felt like me, maybe I wouldn't fight the paranoia. I've taken ownership of my disease, but I know those voices aren't mine."

"You have to stay mentally fit to be able to differentiate between what they're saying and what's a part of you?"

He nodded, his look appreciative. She understood. "Even now, they're trying to tell me that I imagined everything and you're all out to use me and I should run. But since I've been in here and put my ankle up and eaten, they're not as...loud."

"How loud do they get?"

"A cacophony. Deafening. The last time it got that bad was after Lillian's death, but I still don't go out much. A shopping mall taxes my nerves. I go to the same grocery store each time. I don't make friends easily, and forget relationships. I've learned to live with it and that's the most important thing."

A heavy blanket of sympathy draped over her shoulders. He'd finally been invited into the inner sanctum of his daughter's life, surrounded by people who knew his challenges. The Synod would likely wipe his mind, leaving Gray back in his isolated world—and with a new dose of mental unbalance.

He piled his empty cans together on the floor and drained his water bottle. "I'm going to run outside for a minute and then I'd better get some rest, if you don't mind taking first shift. But, Armana, you need to rest, too. I will take a shift of watch."

He rose in a smooth move, wincing only slightly at the stiffness that had set in.

She would've argued about him taking a shift, but lack of sleep wouldn't do her any good. Gray's senses might not be as acute as hers, but she'd be right next to him.

She finished her chicken and beans. A nice rabbit would've been better, but she didn't want to leave Gray to hunt. They couldn't risk a fire to cook, which he'd need. Her, too. Unless she was in wolf form, she preferred her dinner rare, not raw.

Setting up the cots took two minutes. The blankets would be welcome. Summer nights in and around Freemont this time of year didn't dip below fifty-five or sixty degrees, but trying to sleep made it feel colder.

By the time she'd arranged the wool blankets and pulled them back, Gray had returned.

"That looks almost comfortable."

She chuckled. "I do what I can." She stayed by the cot as he sat down. "Do you need help getting your shoes off?"

He hesitated, laying his crutches down. "Do you think that's a good idea?"

"I don't anticipate getting discovered. The rogues seem to have extensive resources, but they weren't tracking Declan's car, and I doubt they know about this place."

"I don't want to hinder an escape. I'm enough of a drain on you."

She stood over him, too close really, and gazed at him. The anguish in his eyes made her want to comfort him. Before she could stop herself or tell herself what a bad idea it was, she stroked his face.

Oh…sweet Mother Earth. The gentle scrape of stubble under her fingers opened a vault of need she hadn't known she possessed.

He was human, but he was male.

The upset in his gaze fused with heat until his walnut eyes simmered with desire.

She brought her other hand up to cup his face. He felt so good. Rough, soft, warm. Suddenly her whole body wanted to know what he felt like.

Bending, she was scared he'd put a stop to what she intended. But his gaze fell to her lips and he planted his hands on her hips.

Their lips touched. A light press that deepened until they parted their lips at the same time. Their tongues tangled.

All of the wants she'd shoved away roared back. Her belly clenched. Heat bloomed between her thighs. Gray released her waist only to scoot across the cot until his back hit the wall with his legs hanging over the other side. He hadn't stretched out before she'd kissed him, leaving room for her to straddle him.

There were so many reasons this was wrong, but for now, she couldn't think any of good enough to stop. She sank onto his lap as they devoured each other.

He brushed her shirt up as he tunneled his hands underneath. His shaft was hard under his pants, but if she ground down, she glimpsed the release he could give her.

His touch crept higher until he cupped her breasts. They were heavy, achy. She arched into him, the move breaking their kiss.

She dragged in a deep breath.

Gray kissed down her neck, sending shivers down her back. She ground down harder.

"We should stop," he said in a ragged voice.

"I know," she answered. When he nibbled a path to her collarbone, she groaned. "I haven't felt like this in so long, Gray. I don't want to stop."

"Me neither." He released her breasts and moved to her waistband. Her fly was flipped open.

"Yes," she hissed. Rocking against his length with so many barriers between them was maddening.

With her legs spread on either side of his, she feared he couldn't get to her sex. But Gray was resourceful and determined.

He wedged his hand between her and her shorts material. When his fingers hit her slick folds, he growled her name.

She cried out and ground into him. His other hand was trying to lift her shirt and she helped him by rolling up. He yanked down her bra and caught a nipple between his teeth.

She was lost in the sensation. So good. So right. So long since she'd had release.

Back and forth, up and down, she rocked, seeking her finish. He held her in his strong arms and a sense of safety descended over her. He had her.

He managed to switch angles and keep working her clit while he inserted a finger.

"More," she gasped.

He thrust and inserted another finger. She slammed her hands against the wall on either side of his head. He licked and kissed her breasts and she rode his hand. Her hair swung behind her, and imagining the picture they made on the cot stoked the heat inside of her into a blaze.

The tension in her uncoiled in a fiery blast. "Gray!" She shook, her orgasm taking over.

He held her until she was done. When she opened her eyes, he gazed at her from under hooded eyelids.

The tightness of his face wasn't from stress this time. He hadn't released and was almost shaking from the effort. But she sensed he wasn't taking things further until he knew what she wanted.

She was a shifter. She wanted more.

Grabbing his wrist and withdrawing his hand, she held his gaze as she wrapped her fingers around the zipper of her shorts and tugged down.

He sucked in a breath. She backed off and they wiggled around until he was lying flat. His shirt had ridden up to show a delectable stretch of skin and a trail of hair that disappeared behind his fly. The broad tip of his cock pushed open his loosened fly. She perched on the edge of the cot and unzipped him. He sprang free.

"I want this," she said, taking him in her hand.

"Whatever you want." His voice was low and rough, just like his hands.

She stood up and swiped off her shirt. It'd be easier for her to get undressed, but he wrestled off his shirt. When his hands landed on his pants, she stayed him with a shake of her head.

She reached down to yank them past his ass. He clocked her moves with a predatory stare she hadn't thought a human could make. When his gaze landed on her freed breasts, she let them sway as she shimmied his pants off of him.

"Armana."

In one smooth move, she straddled him again, hovering over his straining erection. He clamped down on her hips but didn't move her. He waited.

She fisted him, placing him at her entrance, and sank onto him. It'd been so long since she'd been intimate on this level. Her body gripped him like she was afraid he'd withdraw.

His hands loosened and his groan matched hers. He filled her, a pressure she'd missed terribly. She had orgasmed once already, but nothing stroked the right spots like a male. And she had one under her.

She set a languid pace, not knowing how long he could last. From his clenched face, he was concentrating on not coming too early.

She leaned over him, one hand holding herself up on the side of the cot, the other on his chest. The angle stimulated her clit against him as he stroked in and out of her.

He braced his weight on his good leg and sat up to knead her breasts and roll her nipples between his fingers.

She was getting close to another peak. He took over, thrusting into her. She was helpless against him and it was exactly what she wanted.

"Armana, I can't hold back any longer."

The scrape of his voice was enough to topple her over the edge. She cried out and shuddered, her climax washing over her. His fingers dug into her as he breathed her name. He went rigid and tossed his head back, his teeth clenching as he emptied himself inside of her. They strained with each other, scraping every ounce of pleasure they could.

Their scents mingled. He couldn't smell it, but she could. It was…pleasant. More than pleasant. It felt familiar, real.

He relaxed back onto the cot, hugging her to him as he lay flat. He didn't radiate a satisfied afterglow. She didn't either. What they'd done was an urgent form of support and mutual attraction. But it would complicate their life.

Under her ear, his heart hammered a steady beat. He stroked her bare back. She might get chilly in a few minutes, but for now, she was surprised steam wasn't rising from them.

"I feel like you're thinking what I'm thinking," she said.

He chuckled. "That this was great, I want to do it again, and oh my God, what about our kids?"

She giggled. The weight of the last two decades slipped away, but new weight was piled in its place. "Yes." She propped herself up on his chest. "I don't know how they'd take it."

"They're going to take my memories, Armana. I might not remember any of this in a week or a month." He massaged circles in her back that were deceptive in their normalcy, as if nothing was wrong. "I don't want to forget you, but if I don't have to tell Cassie and make her worry, then I won't. I'm sorry."

"You have nothing to be sorry for. I don't relish telling my son who hasn't completely forgiven me that I'm sleeping with his mate's dad."

"Then this is between us? For now, until we know what's going on?"

She traced her fingers along his jaw, her new favorite hobby. "Tonight is between us. But just know, it's not so I can go laugh about you to anyone. I'm with you like this because you've won me over. I like being with you. And I like sex —with you."

The corner of his mouth hitched. "You might have to tell me a few more times."

They might not have to rotate shifts keeping watch. They were going to be awake. For one night, she threw caution out the window and took what she wanted.

CHAPTER 7

G ray held the door open for Armana with a crutch. She breezed out, giving him a saucy look. He didn't need a shifter's senses to tell him the sway of her hips was exaggerated, and he liked it.

He closed the door and descended the stairs to stand beside her. His gaze caressed her face. "It's going to be hard to pretend we're nothing more than friends with survival in common."

"Yes, it will." Did the sadness in her eyes match his own?

Probably. He couldn't risk Cassie questioning his stability by questioning his decision to sleep—or not sleep—with her mother-in-law. He definitely couldn't risk Armana's relationship with Jace.

Gray didn't care much what Jace thought about him, as long as he didn't try to interfere with his relationship with his daughter. But Armana would need Cassie's good opinion in order to heal the rift between her and her son.

Family drama sucked and Gray wasn't going to leave Armana and their kids to wade through it all while he went back to eating supper alone at his tiny kitchen table, oblivious to the paranormal world around him.

He wanted one more kiss from Armana, but they had to meet the Guardians at the base of the trail. One kiss wouldn't be enough when he'd found pure bliss in her body not an hour ago.

She'd mentioned their scents mingling already because they'd been so close together for the last couple of days, but she hoped the desire would fade as they sweated their way down the trail. Yet they couldn't stop themselves. He'd been in that rickety folding chair and she'd crawled on top of him.

Geez, he felt nineteen again. Old enough to discover the wonders of sex and be able to do something about it. But they had to hide it from their children like they were nothing more than teens hiding from their parents.

His ankle felt better after a night of moderate rest. It'd been propped up, even during all the...activity. The food hadn't been tasty, but it'd been more than edible and he started down the trail recharged, with no whispers in his head.

Armana stayed behind him like when they'd come up the trail. The narrow dirt path was wide enough for his feet, and the terrain was flat enough for his crutches to find purchase.

They worked their way down slowly. Armana didn't prod him on. It was like they were both resisting the end to their forced rendezvous. Birds chirped around them and the canopy of leaves saved them from the worst of the sun's rays. The parking lot was almost in sight.

"Jace?" Armana sidled around Gray without disturbing his trek. "There are two of them waiting for us and one is Jace."

Gray increased his pace. Armana wasn't going far from him, but both of them wanted to know if Jace's presence meant the cause of the danger had been removed.

As the trees thinned close to the trailhead, another vehicle came into view. A black SUV, like what the Guardians preferred to drive. Jace came around the front, his icy gaze landing on them immediately.

Jace nodded to someone in the direction of the car Armana had ditched. Gray ducked his head to see what was going on without losing his footing. An unfamiliar man was jimmying the lock on the driver's side. A triumphant look crossed his face and he opened the door. After he got in, the engine started and he drove off.

The bodies had to be smelling by now. Or maybe not. Gray didn't know anything about dead bodies. Did shifters have their own decomposition timeline?

Armana crossed to Jace, her arms folded, but instead of seeming standoffish or defensive, Gray thought it looked she was trying not to tackle him with a hug. "Jace. Is it over?"

Jace inclined his head, his expression grim. "It is."

$\mathcal{A}$rmana rolled to her side and dragged the comforter over her. Then kicked it back off. She sighed and changed positions to her other side.

She couldn't sleep. In her small square room with only one dresser and a two-foot-by-two-foot closet, there was nothing else to do on these restless nights.

She knew what she wanted to do. But Gray was in the guest bedroom in Jace's cabin.

It was over. She should be at peace, but she wasn't, not while Gray's fate hung in the balance. Paralleling that concern was her pride in Jace and his ability to pursue the flesh traders and shut them down.

Her son had to leave soon to track down the victims who had been sold before the Guardians had caught up with the traders and "cleaved through them like butter," to quote Jace. He also thought this wasn't the end of the trouble they'd face. He suspected the trafficking ring had burrowed into their people, using greed and power to spread like a disease.

Of course there'd be more. There were always more bad

guys to chase. More rogues going feral. The eternal struggle to keep their people's secrets. Sometimes she missed her role in it all, when she'd been useful to Bane. To keep watch over his pack, he'd often relied on her observations—which mates were arguing, whose young would leave to start packs of their own, which pups were simply hotheads or actively fomenting discord—as well as her advice on how best to use the information she provided.

As technology had advanced, she'd embraced it to communicate with other packs, essentially running background checks on all new arrivals wishing to becoming members of the pack—or those who'd suddenly left for other packs. She liked to think she'd laid the foundation for the current ways packs connected to disseminate information.

Talking to Gray gave her some of that level of importance, of being *needed*, back. The intimacy was another part of her past she missed.

If her son ever found out… It's not that she wasn't an adult and couldn't have sex with who she wanted. They were shifters and they relished the skin they were born in. It was that it had the potential to hurt Cassie, and she knew it, and that was what Jace wouldn't take lightly. He might see it as a slight against him and how much she really cared for him when she seduced Gray within a day of knowing him.

She couldn't deny how much she'd hurt her son when she'd abandoned him to the human prison system and hadn't even stopped in for a visit. When he'd been arrested, she'd taken Maggie, shuttered the windows, and unplugged her phone. He'd be justified doing the same to her if he found out about her and Gray.

Swinging her legs over the edge of the bed, she sat up. Might as well go for a run. The grounds weren't silent during the night. The Guardians had incorporated vampire trainees, but a gym with barracks had been built on another part of the property to keep the night and day creatures functioning without disturbing the much-needed rest of either.

She kept on her nightshirt and walked through the quiet lodge. Hanging her top on a hook by the front door, she waited to shift until she got outside. Flowing into her wolf, she stretched on her haunches, then took off at an easy pace.

As she loped through the trees, up and over hills, the fresh night air invigorated her. For so many years, she'd missed this. The freedom. The exhilaration of physical feats her human form couldn't accomplish.

Picking up her speed, she bounded through the woods, keeping her senses open for danger, whether it was from rogues like what Jace and the other Guardians hunted or the random camper popping up unexpectedly.

She detected nothing.

She slowed.

She turned and trotted back in the direction she'd come and thought about the real issue keeping her awake. Gray was safe. She'd been around long enough that she knew no matter how much Commander Fitzsimmons argued for Gray's dependability, the Synod would adhere to the one major rule they existed under.

No humans shall learn of their existence. Only mates were given a pass, and that had been a recent development. Some members of the former government that Commander Fitzsimmons helped overthrow had hunted human mates. Species purity, they'd claimed. Keep our bloodlines strong, they'd touted.

Bane had detested human mates. More to protect, more mouths to feed who couldn't hunt for themselves. It didn't help that many human mates were females and Bane had been a male of his time, complete with many of the stereotypes. She was grateful Jace had been too young when Bane died to remember any of Bane's complaints and insults toward human mates.

They hadn't talked about Bane and Keve since they'd reunited. When Jace was younger, he'd asked questions. Armana had answered succinctly until Jace's curiosity was sated or he'd gotten discouraged and quit asking.

The trip back took longer. She must've covered a couple of winding miles and now she meandered.

Her head wasn't clear, but she felt better and maybe could get some sleep. She wove through the cabins. No one was up and moving. The security patrols had stayed out of her way. They'd know it was her, and a shifter going for a midnight run was nothing unusual.

She was almost to the lodge when footsteps crunching on the gravel disturbed the night. She listened, but security wasn't rushing to handle the situation.

Without changing forms, she made an arc around the lodge. A long figure strolled along the unpaved road leading away from the lodge. Gray had his head tipped back, going slow on his crutches, like he was gleaning information from the stars.

She decided against changing back to her other form. Her nudity wouldn't keep a relaxed atmosphere between them, and after their flight for survival, he should be moderately accustomed to her wolf.

He whipped around when she was feet away. The surprise on his face was almost comical when it melted into relief.

"Armana." He put his hand on his chest. "I think I was an inch away from a heart attack." His voice was low, like he didn't want to upset the peace surrounding them. "Couldn't sleep, either?"

He continued his walk. She fell in beside him.

"Jace said the commander wants to see me in the morning. He wasn't...hopeful."

She wished she could express how critical it was for their people to maintain their strict standards of safety and secrecy. But it'd fall flat. He wasn't a threat to them. He could be, unknowingly, but then they all could.

He was a person, someone they all cared about. In her short time with him, she'd come to see him as...a friend? More than a friend, of course, with how they'd behaved last night. But she could so easily rely on him.

It'd been so long since she'd had a partner in life. She didn't need one, but it was nice.

It'd been so long since she'd had a friend. A real friend. During the last twenty years, she'd kept all her acquaintances at arm's length. She'd gone to birthday parties, baby showers, and even a wedding or two. She'd attended office retirements and going-away bashes, but in each instance, if she hadn't attended, it would've gone unnoticed.

She hadn't been important to anyone except Maggie, and while it was still true, Maggie had her own mate, her own life, and was making her own friends.

Walking with Gray tonight was more than nice. It reminded Armana that she needed to get back into the world. She needed to matter again.

She'd gone from young and idealistic to a leader's mate to a mother to...nothing. A shadow that drifted through other people's worlds and barely made them blink.

Good thing she'd stayed in her wolf form. Tears might moisten her eyes and Gray might ask her what was wrong. She wasn't confident she could tell him without sobbing.

She hadn't cried since the night she'd buried her mate and son. The other half of her soul had gotten ripped away from her and only desperation had helped her survive it.

Her need to survive was over. The only choice was to wither away from her nothingness or thrive.

The only problem was she didn't know how to do either one.

* * *

GRAY PUSHED his eggs around his plate. He should eat but food tasted like ash and his stomach was clear about its lack of desire for sustenance.

Cassie was doing the same on his right. Her mate had shoveled his food in and cleaned up his spot. Jace was in the other room, cleaning and gathering his equipment. Gray suspected Jace was giving him time with Cassie.

Gray would've rather stayed somewhere else last night and let the couple have their personal reunion in private. Cassie and Jace had disappeared for a couple of hours after he was done at the lodge. By the time they'd gotten back, Gray had made himself scarce, holing himself up in the guest room with a book.

He hadn't seen a word of it even though he'd stared at it for hours. The voices had bugged him.

They don't want you here.

You're a nuisance.

Crazy old man.

That voice he hated the most. It had popped up after he turned forty-five. He had that damn voice to thank for his rigid workout regimen. He'd made it through three decades with his disease, but that voice grew along with his fear of truly becoming a crazy old man.

At least his daughter wouldn't be alone, no matter what happened to him. Cassie had found herself a good man...a good shifter. Jace looked like a thug who'd jump you for your wallet and keys. But he was a levelheaded young man. Cassie had explained the rash decision he'd made when he was younger that had landed him in prison. As a father to a young girl, Gray couldn't hold it against the guy for what he'd done.

If Jace thought trouble could come at them again, Gray hoped the powers that be listened to him. Selfishly, it also meant he could hold on to his memories longer, be around his daughter more, and...be close to Armana.

Leaving bothered him. Forgetting this beautiful place with its supernatural creatures who took care of his daughter and regular people like him, not being a full part of Cassie's life, tore him in two. All he'd gone through the last few days he'd do over again because for the first time since she was a little girl, he'd had a solid role in her life. He knew *her*, not the Cassie she orchestrated for his benefit.

A mournful sigh pulled him out of his thoughts.

"Peanut?"

She placed her fork next to her plate and propped her cheek in her hand with her elbow on the table. "This sucks, Dad."

He smiled and hoped it didn't look as empty as it felt. "I know. And if we go back to the way it was before, just know that I'll take whatever you can give me. I might not understand why I can't visit here or see your home. I'll try to understand why you don't visit often, but it doesn't matter. Having you safe has always been my priority."

In those frantic days when they'd been living off the grid, her safety had been paramount. One reason his condition had deteriorated so badly was because the reality of raising her on his own had made his mind buckle.

Her eyes glistened. "God, Dad. You know I'm not an emotional person, but this is killing me. I like having you around and it doesn't seem fair."

Tears broke free and rolled down her cheek. She swiped at them but ended up burying her face in her hands.

Gray expected Jace to rush in, but his commitment to giving them space was strong. Gray scooted his chair around and gathered Cassie to him, holding her like he'd done when her mom had died.

He didn't bother blinking back his own tears. Cassie had nailed it. It wasn't fair. He'd found the woman of his dreams, had the prefect child, and within months he'd lost them both. Years later, he'd gotten his daughter back, only to partially lose her again. The only solace he took in any of it was that it wasn't his mind that had failed him this time.

But there was the apprehension that it'd fail him afterward, when it was critical he maintain the status quo. For his daughter's sake.

He clasped his hands around her shoulders. Her sobbing decreased until she fell quiet. They hugged each other for several minutes before Jace cleared his throat from the kitchen entrance.

"Time to go." Jace's gaze was glued to Cassie and his arms were crossed. He wanted to go to his mate.

Gray mouthed *thank you*. Jace ducked his head.

As if Gray needed more things to lose, he'd also miss getting to know the real Jace. How critical his job was. It wasn't just some cushy security job. He was dedicated to his people, and he loved Cassie. His protectiveness had always been apparent but getting to witness them move around each other in their home and see how relaxed and ready to smile Cassie was around Jace was a special treat for a father who worried about his daughter.

"Ugh." Cassie straightened. "I'm a mess."

He was about to say no one would notice, but nothing was missed around here. On his walk with Armana last night, his voices had taunted him that they were being watched. Gray had almost laughed at the irony. Of course they were being watched. These beings didn't miss anything.

He stuck with "I'm sure they'll understand."

Cassie nodded and wiped her face off. She rose and went to the sink to splash water on her face. Gray went to stand beside Jace. He had no items to pack, no luggage. The sweats and T-shirt he was wearing were borrowed.

His ankle felt better but he walked with a limp. He should be using crutches, but they were borrowed, too.

They all walked together down to the lodge. The birds and the wind sweeping through the canopy of leaves produced a more cheerful sound than any of them could've.

Jace held the door open for them. Cassie led the way, taking it slow. His midnight stroll had been a setback for his healing, but he hadn't wanted the crutches with him. Today's trek across uneven ground wasn't helping his ankle mend, but Gray's worries were elsewhere.

His world brightened when Armana emerged from the top of a stairwell. Her half smile was encouraging, but it also said she'd be here to help when he couldn't.

Would the people tampering with his memories be able to see them? He didn't want to get Armana in trouble, or embarrass her.

She'd be so embarrassed, old man. You look like you could be the father of everyone here.

Couldn't his voices leave him alone for the day?

Armana fell in step beside him and Jace caught up with Cassie.

"Thanks for coming," Gray said.

"You don't mind? I wasn't exactly invited."

"Consider this my invitation. You saved me too many times to be left out." And that was the truth.

She wasn't one of the Guardians, she was only the mother of one of them. Just like he was the father of one of their mates. But they were involved. They'd been forced to be involved and this was their penance. He wanted her strength. And a few more moments to soak up her presence.

Jace stopped in front of a solid wood door and knocked.

Gray didn't hear if there was a reply, but Jace opened the door and ushered them all in.

Commander Fitzsimmons was seated behind a sturdy desk full of papers, computers, and various pieces of electronics. His expression could be carved out of stone, except for the subtle lift of a brow as he eyed them. "Since you're all here, I'm assuming you've guessed the Synod's decision."

Jace let out a curse and Cassie's shoulders fell.

Gray rested his hand on her back. "The last thing I want is to be a security risk. If this is the way of your people, I won't protest."

The commander's expression slipped, revealing a stroke of compassion. A blink later it was gone. "I tried to explain the situation to them. How steady and reliable you've been." His jaw clenched. "Then I pleaded the safety of the procedure with regard to your mind, but they say the memories will be essentially locked up. It won't tamper with your brain in any way."

Cassie's brow furrowed. "So, what, he won't remember the last three days?"

"The last four," the commander answered. He pinned Gray with his no-nonsense stare. "We'll take you home, let you get changed so we can take the clothing back. Your front door has already been fixed and the kitchen cleaned up. I had Doc call into your job as your doctor to clear you from the work you missed. You hurt your leg and the meds made your brain foggy. That'll be the story."

"When can I talk to him next?" Cassie asked.

"When he calls you. Until he makes contact, we stay out of it. It's better for his mind that way."

Because he'd be trying to process the loss of time and why his leg hurt. What a mess. But...it was doable and he was hanging on to that.

"Okay. I'm ready."

CHAPTER 9

*A*rmana sank onto her bed, her head in her hands.

That had been rough. She massaged her temples, struggling to keep her tears at bay. She'd expected a sad event, but not how personally devastated she'd feel losing Gray.

She'd held it together while Gray had disappeared into his bedroom and emerged with an armload of clothing to hand over. Commander Fitzsimmons had been true to his word. The door had been fixed and the kitchen returned to its original state. It'd probably been done the same night to keep nosey neighbors from growing alarmed.

Gray had shaken hands with Jace, then given her a perfunctory hug with a longing look that she'd understood to her soul. He'd wanted a proper goodbye and so had she, but they'd been restricted to a good-natured pat on the back. The departing hug between Cassie and Gray had been heartbreaking.

Armana had left with Jace and Cassie so Commander Fitzsimmons and the shifter who manipulated memories could work on Gray. They'd said Gray would sleep long and hard and wake up disoriented. But the memory shifter had left clues, like a prescription and a doctor's note from Doc. His new pill bottle and his old were nestled back in the cupboard with his vitamins. They'd dirtied dishes to set by the sink.

They'd even visited Dr. Sodhi and tidied up his memory of Gray's last appointment. How thorough.

A knock at the door caught her attention.

Jace stood outside, his eyes narrowed on her. "Can I come in?"

"You don't have to ask."

He stepped inside but didn't take the spare chair she kept by the wall. As if she ever got company. She used the chair to tie her shoes on; that was its only purpose.

"You took today kind of hard," he said. His arms were crossed as he leaned against the doorframe.

"Yeah. Gray's a good man. I feel bad for Cassie."

"Nothing's going to change between them."

"Isn't it?" Armana snapped, then sighed. "Sorry. He lives a solitary life and he loves that girl of yours. I wish he could be involved more. It's not like she has forever with him."

"None of us are guaranteed forever."

She stared at her son. When'd he become so hard? Prison? His job? Had breaking up families when he terminated rogues become such a common occurrence? "I know that. As nearly immortal beings, we know how long life is when we lose someone we love."

"Which is what brings me here." He pushed off the door and wandered in. "You two seemed close."

"Did we." It purposely didn't sound like a question. It was all she could do not to be defensive, and she didn't want to go two steps back with her son.

"Yep." His icy stare was on her, but she didn't wither under it. He got it from both her and his father, and Bane had never been able to intimidate her. She refused to give her son the power. It wasn't healthy between them. "I'm fond of Gray. He's a good man, and I'm as worried as Cassie."

"Why?"

Seriously? "Because I care about people, Jace."

He snorted and when she shot him a hard look, he clarified, "I'm trying to get past how easily you dumped me when I made a mistake. I'm trying to understand the reason why, and after that bastard who killed Dad almost got Maggie, I'm coming around. But this isn't about our history." He walked to her dresser where her ceremonial *gladdus* was set on the top. "What I'm asking is, have you dated since Dad died?"

Jace couldn't know. She and Gray had smelled like each other the morning he'd picked them up, but there'd been another valid reason. Afterward, the desire they'd felt for one another had been buried by anxiety and relief that the danger was gone.

Right?

"Even in those rare moments I thought about dating again, I had kids to worry about. When Maggie moved out…" Armana lifted a shoulder. "I was preparing to move and start a new job and it seemed pointless."

She caught a glimpse of something rare in Jace's eyes: empathy. It gave her hope that one day they could grow close again.

"You seemed different around Gray."

She answered honestly. "I haven't been able to make friends and he would've been a good one."

"Yeah," he said gruffly. "Cassie's napping, but I think she just wanted to cry in peace. Keeping our life from her dad has been hard. And now she knows what's she missing, so…"

"Go be there for her."

"Yeah." He stared at the dagger. "I was thinking that maybe you should go visit Maggie for a while."

Armana cocked her head. What the hell brought that up? "Maggie's busy with work."

"So am I, and that's why I think it'd be good for you to get away for a bit."

She narrowed her eyes on him. He didn't smell like he was lying, but he wasn't saying everything. "What's going on, Jace?"

He finally glanced away, his gaze bouncing everywhere but her. "When I met you guys at the trailhead, I thought that I...that maybe I...you know, that you two..."

Wasn't this how they'd felt during that first birds and bees talk? An awkward conversation neither wanted to have? "And for argument's sake, what if we had...you know..." Sweet Mother Earth, she couldn't say it either.

"I mean, it'd be weird, but you're both adults. Whatever. But now it's different. Cassie can still see and talk to him and you can't, and I'll be out on missions."

Armana straightened, her shoulders squared. "And you don't want to worry about me on top of your mate."

His stony gaze finally landed on her. "If you two...then he's different to you. And I can't have you risk his mental status trying to contact him again."

The thought of staying with Maggie for the next several weeks shredded her nerves. She'd just lost Gray and had hoped to be around to support Cassie. If she went to Lobo Springs, she'd be alone again. She'd love to hang with her daughter, but Maggie was working and newly mated. Not to mention Armana had a hard time being in Lobo Springs for any amount of time. There was nothing like a stroll down memory lane to summon the pain and grief of all she'd almost lost herself to.

She steeled herself. What she said next was going to hurt

them both. "Jace, you of all people should know that I can sever ties with someone I care about. I think I'll be fine here."

Jace flinched and blinked. There were the two steps back. She hadn't sounded cavalier, but he was still recovering from her abandonment. There were no rules that said a kid had to be a child for their parent to hurt them, and she'd just ripped off the bandage.

"No contact at all, Armana. None."

She bit her lip at his use of her first name. She hadn't been Mom for a long time. It was like he tested it out once in a while, then went back to her first name. Pretty soon, she'd be Mrs. Miller. Or Troye, if she went back to using her real name.

"I understand the importance, my son. I was making a point—"

"Then we're done here." He stormed out.

She closed her eyes and dragged in a shaky breath.

GRAY BLINKED AWAKE. Light was fading in his room.

Was it morning? It didn't feel like morning. The shadows were long, leaving the area dim. The birds outside chirped a chorus at sunrise, but now they were relatively quiet. It was evening.

He rolled up to a seat and winced. Prodding his temples did nothing for his pounding headache. Was that the reason he'd napped?

Grunting from the effort, he swung his legs down and stood. He barked a yell and flopped back down. Bringing his left leg up, he lifted the hem of his jeans. Purple and green bruising circled his ankle.

He frowned. Those were fading bruises and he didn't remember getting injured in the first place.

I sprained my ankle and the meds knocked me out. I've called into work and will return when I feel better.

His brow creased as those two sentences ran through his head like a script.

I sprained my ankle and the meds knocked me out. I've called into work and will return when I feel better.

"Okay, got it," he muttered. What meds?

He rose to his feet, keeping his weight off his hurt foot. Limping across the room, his gaze snagged on the stairs.

Good Lord, how was he getting down the stairs with the sprain? No wonder he'd relied on pain meds. Why hadn't he gotten crutches?

He grabbed the railing, hopped down a stair and sat down. Scooting down the stairs on his butt would get the job done, but he scowled back at the flight.

Why hadn't he gotten crutches?

As he made his way to the kitchen, he relied on his injured limb more and more. He was healing and it wasn't as bad as he first thought.

But when had he fallen?

His phone was on the counter. Why had he left it there?

He looked at the screen. No messages, no missed calls.

No surprise.

He went into recent calls. There was one to work from this morning. He had zero memory of it.

I've called into work and will return when I feel better.

Yeah, okay. Work tomorrow. Could he do the whole shift on his feet? His boss was usually understanding when employees weren't functioning at 100 percent and would find something for him to do sitting down.

So...

He inhaled and leaned on the counter. His stomach rumbled. Checking the time, his brows lifted. It was almost eight p.m. Had he missed lunch in addition to supper?

His pill.

He went to the cupboard and grabbed a glass for water and his pill bottle. His hand stalled. Two bottles were next to each other. When had he gotten a refill?

He checked the date. Three days ago.

He shook his head and took his dose. Anxiety climbed up his spine. Memory loss wasn't a hallmark of schizophrenia. He was confident in the signs of a relapse and lately he'd been...

What? What had he been feeling recently?

Bored. Lonely. Those were standard. Either way, he was hungry. Might as well eat since he couldn't answer what he didn't know.

He rummaged around the fridge. Opening the milk, he didn't have to get close to smell it. Uck. He set it on the counter to drain and throw away later. Leftover meatloaf. That'd be a good meal for the evening.

He searched for the container. Dammit. Had he eaten it in his pain-med stupor?

Switching his attention to the cabinets, he located the empty and cleaned container the meatloaf had been in. Only it was in the wrong cupboard. Gray set it on the counter next to the milk and crossed his arms. How many days had he lost? He'd checked the time, but not the date.

Pulling up the home screen on his phone, he swallowed hard at the date. He couldn't remember the last four days. What medication had he been on?

I threw out the bottle and decided not to take more.

The thought rose like it was summoned, only he wasn't sure he'd been the one to recall it. How odd. His voices weren't usually so...foreign.

Finding a loaf of bread that was still good, he tossed a couple of slices into the toaster and crossed his arms as he glowered at the small appliance.

Whatever he'd done to hurt himself, he couldn't do it again. Whatever medication he'd taken for pain, he couldn't do it again. The risk to his mental health wasn't worth it.

CHAPTER 10

 *hree weeks later...*

GRAY WOKE up on his back and stared at the ceiling. He had another round of snooze before he had to get ready for work. Usually, he set his alarm early so he wouldn't have to rush and get in a negative headspace. Sometimes, he'd meditate if the voices were quiet enough to keep it from an exercise in futility.

His dreams… Every one had been full of pretty blue eyes and a sense of acceptance that he coveted. He awoke hard and achy like he'd never experienced before.

Swinging his legs down, he scrubbed his face. If he started dreaming about meeting a woman who'd accept him as he was, he'd certainly succumb to the disease. There was being teased, and then there was torment. He could delude himself about his loneliness, lie and say it was for the best, that it was better to be alone than to get close to someone who'd only run when they learned about the voices and his previous breakdown.

The woman. The freedom of being with her. He couldn't go there.

There'd been a cabin in his dreams, too, and it wasn't one he remembered from his time living in the woods outside of Freemont.

Brushing off the dreams the best he could, he got ready for work. But today he packed running clothes for after his shift. He'd started running again a couple of days ago. With his job and health insurance, he got a discounted membership to a gym and used it to lift. It'd been a good place to test his ankle. And if he had to endure another weekend of reruns and reading and being couch-bound, he was going to go crazy and not in a way that had to do with his illness.

Today, he was running outside. He planned to find a trail and enjoy the great outdoors. Since he'd been dreaming about it, he'd give in and give his mind the vacation it was asking for.

His mind had been strangely quiet since he'd woken with four days missing. At work, a voice would whisper the standard *He thinks you don't know what you're talking about* and then leave it at that.

He didn't dare hope that forgetting a chunk of his life had reset his disease to the beginning, when it hadn't been as severe or as easily provoked.

He should've kept that pill bottle.

With his shorts and running shoes packed, he left for work. The day was the same as every day before it. He assisted a family with finding the right tent for camping by the lake.

As he was discussing tent size with the mother, a voice said, *She knows you're sick.*

Gray's brows lifted. His voices had never sounded so...halfhearted.

He sent the family on its way and found another couple to help. His shift was uneventful but ticked by in infinitesimal increments. He wanted to find a trail and go running. Really badly.

Finally, he clocked out. Driving out of town, he had no idea how he'd find a trail. He just kept going.

He should stop somewhere. Freemont was surrounded by lakes of all sizes, and a river cut between Freemont and West Creek. No one who really wanted to hike a trail had to leave city limits. But just any trail wouldn't do today. It was like he'd handed over the control of his car to another power. It should scare him, but finding the right trail was critical.

An hour later, he pulled into an empty trailhead that also functioned as the parking lot for a campground that could only be accessed by hiking.

There. The perfect trail. How'd he known that?

Realization struck him and he stared at the dirt path disappearing into the trees. This must be where he'd gotten hurt.

No, that didn't seem right, but it was the perfect explanation. His subconscious was trying to fill in those missing days.

With a smile that made him glad no one else was around, he got out and went through his warm-up routine. Taking off at an easy gait, he followed the path. It was more rugged than he'd expected. No wonder he'd sprained an ankle. He should be wearing trail shoes.

He kept his pace slower than normal and slowed further when he spotted a rustic cabin.

A jolt of fear went through him, but it was more like an echo of what he'd felt at one time. He must've had his spill here and worried about getting back to his car.

Yeah, that made sense.

What about the eyes as pale as an iced-over lake? His wife's eyes hadn't been blue, so why was he dreaming of a mystery woman with those eyes?

He shook his head and walked the rest of the way to the cabin. Déjà vu grew stronger the closer he got.

"Hello?" he called, just in case. If someone lived here, and the overgrown wildflowers and weeds didn't make him think there was, they had to be used to the occasional hiker happening upon them.

No one answered. He went up the steps and tried the door, jumping when it swung open.

He took a hesitant step inside.

Dust and must was all he smelled, but... It was the feeling. He liked being in here. He didn't want to leave. Perhaps he'd crawled here and was grateful he'd had a shelter over his head?

Could the mystery woman have stumbled upon him and helped him?

That made so much sense. She'd helped him. So many times. He didn't know any of the ways but was more desperate for answers than he'd thought.

Wandering through the sparse building yielded no further clues, just feelings. A flush worked its way up his neck and... Hell, was he turned on?

She must've been something to elicit such a reaction when he couldn't even recall who she was. Had they swapped numbers? He checked his phone. No new contacts.

Dang.

With a sigh, he spun and strode out. He shut the door with purpose but left his hand resting on the knob.

This is over. I have my answers, as much as I'll get.

He couldn't allow a foolish pursuit like this to plague him any longer. Jogging back, he cleared his head. Tomorrow was

Friday. He had the weekend to explore other trails. Should he call Cassie and invite her and Jace over for supper one night?

Stopping in front of his car, he circled around in a three-sixty. This area was so familiar. Perhaps it was the call of the wild. He'd loved the woods and hiking, but after his breakdown, he hadn't dared step foot in them, never knowing if it'd act as a trigger.

But he looked forward to exploring more trails. The woods called to him. They were peaceful, in a different way than how he'd constructed his uneventful life. Tie it in with self-care and the lack of paranoia he'd experienced over the last two weeks, and he just might have found a new hobby for himself. Hiking.

* * *

"OH, HEY," Cassie greeted. "How's it going?"

Just like the last three weeks, Armana sensed a deeper meaning to Cassie's casual question. Each time, Armana edited her actions and anything she said to disguise how often she thought about Gray.

"It's going well," Armana said. "Have a fun night planned?"

They were outside the lodge, and Cassie was dressed in cotton shorts and a purple tee.

"Jace is bringing the car around. We're going to Dad's for supper."

Armana forced a smile. "How lovely. Has it been difficult for you, pretending…?"

Cassie blew out a breath. "So hard. It's not just pretending that nothing happened to Dad, but doing it in a way where he doesn't think I'm hiding something."

"How is he?" Armana had been dying to ask that each time she saw Cassie. It had required much restraint not to chase after her, repeating the question until she got a damn answer.

But restraint she had. She'd stayed away from Gray's part of town. She hadn't suddenly started shopping in the store he worked at or taking evening strolls in his neighborhood. But trying to avoid thinking about him proved useless. His well-being and safety were as much her priority as seeing after her son and his mate, or her daughter.

The pathetic part was that they all could take care of themselves and she had nothing to do. She'd taken to running a lot. Running her wolf through the woods around the lodge was doable, but there were getting to be so many Guardians and their mates that it often wasn't the exercise in solace she hoped for.

Jace pulled out of the garage and idled around to them. He nodded at her. Armana loved seeing how his gaze softened when it landed on Cassie, but did it have to cut glass when he looked at her?

He'd been gone a lot for work, so they hadn't had many chances to chat. She wanted to make progress in their relationship, but for him, Cassie came first, then work, then... well, she didn't know where she stood.

Perhaps she *should* visit Maggie. Get out of her funk by getting out of her minimal routine. Then she'd go job hunting. She hadn't worked in West Creek before, and since she needed a place where people didn't know her or her age, that'd be a good place to start looking. The commander had hooked her up with new documents and a resume to show that she was thirty-five-year-old Armana Miller with nothing but adequate computer knowledge and office skills.

Let the job search begin. But first, she might pick a trail along the river to run tomorrow. It'd be good for her. Get her out of her rut.

CHAPTER 11

G ray went through the motions of his warm-up as he eyed the trail. This was a new one. He'd stayed in town today, but the trail by the cabin he'd gone to last week was a siren's call. He wouldn't go there more than once a month. Any more frequently and it'd be a sign he was deteriorating. It'd be heartbreaking after celebrating doing so well for the last few weeks.

His dinner last night with Cassie and Jace had gone well. He paused in his stretch and frowned at the ground.

She had been quieter than usual. Even odder had been Jace's participation in the conversation. He'd never sat and said nothing during their visits, but he usually had to be prodded. Gray had learned that the guy's mind was as sharp as his stare, but he wasn't loquacious. Any questions about finances and the stock market and Jace would talk until all of their eyes crossed.

Gray would've asked him why he'd gone into private security instead of the financial industry, but his appearance spoke enough. People would be more willing to trust Gray with all of their money and it'd been close to thirty years since Gray had dealt with numbers beyond his own bank account, and that had been math classes in college.

If Jace opened up shop and promised the savviest investing and highest return, people would assume he had mob connections. And Gray had never heard rumors of the mob in Freemont.

A few other cars were in the parking lot. It was early morning on a Sunday. Gray chose this time because the running paths would be quiet and the heat of the day wouldn't chase him back to his AC.

His gaze landed on a black sedan. There was nothing unique about it, but he stared at it for far too long. A passerby might worry that Gray was going to break into it.

He shook his head and took off. He planned a punishing run for the day. He'd tackled trails all week had taken it slow so he wouldn't injure himself. Today was for a workout.

A poster for a marathon had caught his eye at work. Twenty-six point two miles were twenty too many for him, but a half marathon would be cool to work toward. When was the last time he'd committed to something other than keeping his job and not losing his mind?

He'd mentioned it to Cassie last night and her genuine smile had boosted his confidence. Yeah, it was time he do something for himself outside the realm of self-care. A steady training schedule fell in line with that, but it was also for him.

Feeding off the invigoration flowing through him, he pushed his pace. He followed the paved path parallel to the river, and the alternating views of glittering blue river and green leafy trees were a balm to his spirit.

He went faster.

A small voice in his mind asked him why he was speeding up until his chest heaved and his lungs burned. The voice was his own, and that lessened the physical exertion. He sucked in air and blew it out, pumped his arms, convincing his tired legs to keep turning over.

He passed only a few other joggers, and they were all heading back to the parking lot. Flying down the path, he maintained the fastest speed he could. When he spotted a woman jogging, her long, lean legs apparent even from the few hundred yards between them, a jubilant cheer echoed in his mind.

Finally.

Without giving himself a chance to wonder why it seemed like he was chasing down a stranger, he closed the distance. She was running at a good clip, but he was faster. He made sure of it.

She must've heard his approach because she slowed to a walk. He was almost to her when she cautiously turned.

Those eyes. The palest of blue and as keen as… How odd. She had eyes almost as crystal blue as Jace's.

But hers glittered as brightly as the river next to them under the bright July sun. Her shirt was a fitted green material. She was nature personified.

"Hey," he wheezed. He should've forced himself to pass her and continue his run. A sweaty, gasping man probably wasn't welcome, or worse, would scare her.

But the look on her face wasn't fear or irritation. Her eyes were wide and her lips parted. Astonished was the best word he could think of.

"H-hi." She tore her gaze away and looked around. But it wasn't the darting look of a woman making sure she wasn't alone with an unknown man who'd charged up on her. Was she looking for someone in particular?

"Gorgeous morning for a run." He fell into step beside her but missed the view of her swaying hips in her black leggings. The neon detail along the seams only highlighted the sensual grace of her movement.

"Yes, it is." Her rich voice filled him with a craving best left alone until he at least knew her name. Those feelings were dangerous for him. He'd get excited about the prospect of a real relationship only to remember he was mentally ill and dread took over.

She glanced at him again with her deer-in-the-headlights look, like he was a car roaring down on her and she wasn't sure which way to run, or if she should. He hoped she didn't.

Wait...she wasn't acting like she knew him. Was she not the one who'd helped him?

"Do we know each other?" He might as well get it over with and not suffer the awkwardness of the *does she know me or doesn't she* question.

She peered at him, concern flitting through her gaze. Great. Was he coming across as pushy, or worse, crazy?

"No, I don't believe we've ever met." Her pace picked up, her stride clipped.

"I'm really sorry. I thought... You're so familiar." He chuckled and tipped his head back to blink at the sky. The color only reminded him of her eyes. "I must've worried you, coming up to you like this."

He was rewarded with a small smile. "No, it's fine. You didn't scare me. How...how do you think we've met before?"

He chuckled, more in derision toward himself than with real humor. "This is going to sound like a stretch, but a few weeks ago, I sprained my ankle so badly I was given pain meds. I was out for days—it was so bad that I don't even remember what happened."

"That's awful," she murmured, staring straight ahead. He should look away before his staring got creepy, but she was breathtaking, and probably too young to be interested in him. The lighter brown tones of her mahogany hair glowed under the sun and her ponytail showed off her graceful neck and strong frame. She carried herself like she wouldn't be scared of him.

He'd better finish his story or she was going to think he was a stalker. "At least I think I found where it happened."

She whipped her head toward him. "What?"

He nodded. Maybe she'd had the same thing happen and could understand how easily he'd forgotten. "I found this trail outside of Freemont a ways, and it was a little rougher than I'm used to. I'm guessing I fell and made my way to this little cabin that was up the trail. I thought maybe I remembered you from that cabin, like maybe you had called an ambulance."

A flush crept into her cheeks and she looked away. "I don't hit the trails that far from home."

"Oh." What else could he say? She wasn't the lady he remembered. But he didn't want to leave. "I thought that since you were out running today, it must've been a small-world thing. I should get back to my run."

Only his legs were shot. Lungs, too. He'd pushed it really hard. A bad way to start a new training program, but he'd been a man on an unknown mission. Or she'd been the proverbial carrot he'd been trying to reach.

That was absurd. He wouldn't have known she would be out here.

"Small world, indeed," she said. "You're all healed now?"

He could fist-pump the sky that she'd opened a new line of conversation. "Much better. I gave it two weeks of solid rest. It complained a little after the first few times I ran."

As if the joint sensed him talking about it, it sent a twinge of pain through his lower leg. He grimaced, bringing her gaze back to him.

"I think I pushed it too hard today, though." How far back to the parking lot was it? He had to walk or run back and since he didn't want any setbacks to his recovery, he'd better not jog.

"It's hurting?" She stopped. "Where are you parked?"

He pointed behind him. "The parking lot next to the marina."

She turned and he spun with her. "I'll walk back with you. So, this trail. Is it one you usually run on?"

"No, that's the weird thing. I've…" He couldn't say he avoided anything close to the woods because he was afraid his paranoia would rage. "I stick to the treadmill. Running was just for fitness. A git-'er-done thing. But this summer, I've rediscovered the refreshing thrill of running outdoors. Picking different trails, bike paths, dirt roads, or sidewalks. It's only been a week since I've been exploring. I'm not letting my sprain-induced blackout stop me."

She smiled, but her eyes were touched with sadness. "That's really great."

How fun would it be to have someone to explore with? He couldn't go down the road of imagining it with her. They'd just met. "I'm Gray, by the way. Gray Stockwell."

Indecision crossed her face one moment and was gone the next. "I'm… Amy. Amy Miller."

He stuck out his hand—after checking that it wasn't gross from sweat. "Nice to meet you. Thanks for walking me back. I feel like I owe you one."

"You don't owe me anything, Gray." There. The way she said it made him feel like they knew each other.

Was that his disease affecting him?

The voices were still subdued, but his paranoia wasn't dependent on the phrases screamed in his head. It was a feeling encouraged by the voices.

The walk back to the parking lot took an hour. He'd run over three miles at what he estimated to be close to a six-and-a-half-minute pace. Not bad for an old man.

Tinges flared in his ankle as they strolled back. He'd take the next couple of days off running. His job required him to be on his feet, so it'd work out. He'd finish mapping out his training plan and pick some places to run while he rested.

"Well, here we are." He hated seeing the parking lot come into view. Amy was easy to talk to. She was in between jobs at the moment and had two grown kids, which surprised him. She must've been a young mother, but he didn't inquire further. He told her about Cassie, and his pride threatened to make him explode with confetti. Amy's throaty laugh would stay with him for days.

"How's your leg?" she asked.

He shrugged. "As long as I don't run for a couple of days, it'll be fine." They reached the edge of the parking lot. Should he ask her out?

"Good. It was nice to meet you." She smiled and started to head in another direction.

"Do you want to get coffee sometime?"

She paused and her brow creased. "I shouldn't…"

"You don't drink coffee?" Because he didn't. The caffeine worked against his calm and he couldn't take the risk.

Her lips quirked. "I don't mind the drinks that are more like desserts."

He tried an easy grin, hoping it didn't look like he was pleading. "We should meet for real dessert then."

She chuckled and brushed a loose tendril of hair behind her ear. "I still shouldn't."

His heart sank straight to his running shoes. "I understand. Either way, it was still nice to meet you, and thank you for the conversation."

He dug his key out of his pocket and concentrated on opening the door and not staring after her.

"I hear O'Donnell's has great cheesecake."

He turned to find she hadn't moved. His grin returned. "I

haven't been there in years." He and Cassie had eaten at the bar and grill once.

He mentally scrolled through his calendar for a date to suggest. Could he wait until next weekend to see Amy again? Then again, he had a couple of nights off from training. Asking to meet her Monday might be too soon, but Friday or Saturday was too far away.

"Are you free Tuesday night? Eight o'clock?" She'd said dessert and he didn't want to push his luck.

"I'll meet you there." This time she did walk away.

Prying his gaze off of the mesmerizing sway of her hips, he climbed into his car. *Play it cool. Play it cool.* His grin had to be hitting each ear, it was so big.

He had a date. He'd started out thinking he knew her, only to want to get to know her, and now they had a chance.

Movement in the rearview mirror caught his eyes and his smile slipped. The dark sedan he'd thought looked familiar was pulling out of the parking lot. Amy was driving it.

Coincidence that he'd thought he recognized both her and the car, and it turned out to be her car?

She's lying to you.

She lied and you're stupid enough to believe her.

He frowned at his steering wheel. His voices had picked a shitty time to increase their volume.

He needed to go home and rest. Self-care. His condition wasn't going to ruin this for him.

* * *

THE O'DONNELL'S parking lot was half full. The supper crowd was filtering out and it was only Tuesday night. The log and stone structure loomed in front of Armana. She glowered at it from the safety of her car.

What the hell was she doing?

She should've let Gray walk himself back to his car, but she'd told herself that it was suspicious he thought she looked familiar. Top it off with him returning to that cabin that haunted her dreams. She'd wake with the memory of what they'd done there, her body heavy and aching for his touch.

So she'd stayed with him all the way back to the parking lot, telling herself she had to determine how much memory he'd retained and if it was returning. It was a bullshit excuse, she saw that in hindsight.

She should've returned, reported to the commander what had happened on the running trail—not in the cabin—and let him decide the next step. But her protective instinct couldn't be overridden. What if the commander tried to tamper with Gray's mind again? No, she couldn't do that to him or Cassie.

But meeting for dessert? What had she been thinking?

She'd been thinking about the disheartened look on his face when she'd turned him down. She'd been preening over how he'd asked her out even though he thought they'd never met, much less already knew each other intimately. She'd been failing at ignoring her own disappointment over not seeing him again and reminiscing over how easy it was to talk to him and how she'd missed him.

Yeah. So that was what she'd been thinking.

"Stupid female," she muttered.

Cassie had even invited her over for dinner tonight and Armana had met with her and eaten, then conjured an excuse about going for an evening run at her favorite trail. Lying like a teenager sneaking around with a forbidden boy.

And doubling her guilt was Jace's absence. Cassie had confided in her that Jace didn't think the trafficking ring had been truly terminated. There were several, of course, because the sale and trade of flesh knew no boundaries or limits, but this one was nastier than others he'd been hunting. It was like they had an unknown advantage.

And there was Cassie's concern that her dad would get dragged into it again. Another reason for Armana to delude herself into thinking that staying close to Gray was a valid plan and not a selfish one.

Gray pulled up in his Impala. He was a few minutes early, but not desperately early like she'd been. She got out and ignored the flutter in her belly. Was she twenty again?

He smiled when he saw her. She'd seen him in workout clothes and Jace's things. Tonight, Gray wore charcoal-gray slacks and a maroon shirt that lightened the brown in his hair and eyes. And the way it stretched across his shoulders only reminded her of how she'd clutched them when she rode him.

A wave of heat rolled through her. Good thing he wasn't a shifter or he'd smell her desire.

He crossed to her and held an arm out like a damn gentleman. These small gestures showed her both how human he was and how far she'd come. When Armana was younger, she'd bare her fangs and snarl at a male trying to be gallant. She would've taken it as a sign he thought she was the weaker sex. Nowadays, she appreciated the gesture for the respect it showed.

Gray hadn't shown anything less than appreciation when she'd helped him through the woods before and after he'd gotten hurt. He didn't marvel over her abilities because she was female. Just because.

Touching him as they walked into the restaurant was all kinds of wonderful. His scent. His solid body under her hands again.

Damn.

She scanned the restaurant as she walked in. Inhaling

deeply, she sifted through the scents. No shifters, thank the Mother.

She could use the excuse she was keeping an eye on Gray, but there'd be consequences to face, from both the commander and the Synod. And Cassie and Jace. What would the Synod do? Lock her up?

Dating humans wasn't forbidden. Armana wasn't planning to reveal their people to him—again. What would happen?

She didn't want to find out. She caught herself from turning and striding back out, but she'd come this far. What if he'd remembered more since Sunday?

Finding out would be prudent and she was here now. They didn't know anyone in the place, so she might as well stay.

After they were seated, they fell back into relaxed visiting, perusing the desserts, picking ones they both wanted to try and swapping them.

When she'd first charged into Gray's house, their relationship—as friends and lovers—had been built on survival, fear for their children, and their own loneliness. Now, she was getting to know more about him, and dammit she liked him. A lot. He was witty, funny, and mature, and she already knew sex with him was amazing.

Her body throbbed, begging her to find relief.

As the workers started sweeping and cleaning tables, Gray glanced at the time on his phone. "I guess they're closing up."

She sighed wistfully. It'd been a good night, and she didn't want it to end. "Yeah, I suppose we should go."

"Yeah." He sounded as regretful as she was.

He paid and they strolled out to her car. Her arm was woven through his like when they'd entered, only her body was pressed against his, her head nearly on his shoulder.

"Can I see you again?" he asked as they stopped by her car door.

It was on her lips to say she couldn't. Shouldn't. But his head was tipped and his lips were so close and all she could think about was what a good kisser he was.

She rose to her tiptoes and planted her mouth on his. He released her arm to wrap his around her waist. Their kiss deepened until she twined her arms around his neck. They were connected, her breasts rubbing against his chest, her needy core suggesting she rock against him.

She softly broke the kiss. "I don't want this night to end."

"Me either." His gaze, steeped in desire, swept over her face. "Do you want to come back to my place?"

"Yes. I'll follow you." *Bad idea, Armana.*

Alarms should be going off. Blaring. But she didn't stop herself. He got in his car, she got in hers, and she followed him. She knew where he lived but he didn't know that.

Her internal warnings were silent. She had the green light to go back to his place. After so many years of depriving herself and her senses, tonight was hers.

CHAPTER 12

*G*ray dipped his head to lick along Amy's graceful collarbone. She writhed under him as he thrust in and out, trying to keep a steady pace when he just wanted to frantically pump away.

He'd let her into the house and asked if she was sure. Her eyes had danced and she'd said, "I'm old enough to know what I want."

He was, too. And they'd both wanted it now and hadn't made it upstairs to his bedroom. She was stretched out on his couch, where he'd ushered her to sit while he got them something to drink, not wanting to seem too forward. He'd brought her home, hoping to continue the date, and of course, as a red-blooded man with an attractive, smart, sexy woman, if things went further… But he hadn't had expectations.

Their glasses of water sat untouched on the end table. Amy had kissed him and things had just progressed. Really fast.

The way she clung to him, like she had a craving and he was the only flavor she wanted. A guy could get used to that.

He knew how she felt. Since he'd dreamed about her pale eyes, then heard her voice, he'd yearned for her.

She twined her long legs around him, her hips rising to meet him. Her hands gripped his shoulders and held him so tightly he couldn't nibble down past her neck. Instead he captured her mouth and caught her moan. Or was that his? He couldn't tell, enraptured by the feel of her slick sex coating him.

Her walls fisted around him and he kissed her harder, hoping to stave off his orgasm long enough to see to hers.

He needn't have worried. She exploded, going rigid in his arms before she shook through her climax. He released right after her, a surge so powerful he was caught between wondering if he'd survive and never wanting it to end.

"Gray," she whispered. "I missed"—she tensed for a heart-beat—"this. I missed this."

"Me, too," he replied honestly. He missed intimacy. He missed being in a relationship. He missed being…normal. It'd been so many years since his disease hadn't steered his life and had the final say in a relationship. Not many women wanted to enter their golden years with a man who might be more work than pleasure.

"What are you thinking about?" Amy stroked his hair.

He adjusted them, slipping out of her and mourning the loss of her heat, until they were nestled into the couch cushions. His backside faced out and she was snuggled between him and the couch back. He'd gladly fall off to keep her comfortable.

How should he answer? Was it too soon for honesty? She might be looking for a good time, or several good times, but not a lasting partnership. He wanted them to last, but he'd only just met her. At the same time, it wasn't fair to either of them to continue growing closer when he only got more invested and she might check out when he revealed his schizophrenia.

"I'm marveling over you." That part was true.

"I do the same with you."

"Really?" He was nothing to marvel at.

"You're genuine, Gray Stockwell. That's hard to find in a man." She laid her hand flat on his chest. His heart thrummed under her touch.

Genuine. Good God, he was anything but. How could he be when he had to hide a huge part of himself?

"My feelings are genuine and I like you, Amy."

She blinked and uncertainty flitted through her expression. "I hear a but in there."

"No buts." He rested his head on the cushion and came to terms with what he had to do. Things hadn't progressed to this level so quickly with other women he dated. They either had "the talk" before sex, or he'd known they were only in it for the bedroom activity and hadn't worried about it.

He and Amy clicked. He had to tell her. "You might be the one with a major reservation. I have schizophrenia."

Her eyes didn't flare wide. She didn't gasp or look away. She brushed her fingers across his jaw. He loved when she did that. "Tell me about it."

He did. The story poured out of him. He'd never been this free recounting his past before. He ended with, "So I'm stable now, but I don't know what my future holds. I try to concentrate on being my healthiest self today so I don't stress as bad about a future breakdown."

"You sound as if it's inevitable."

"I have more hope than I used to. If I'm to believe what I find online, and what my shrink says, it sounds like my future can be as stable as today. The side effects of my medicine might be more pronounced and it'll be harder to maintain this level of physical fitness as I age, but I'm...hopeful. I want to be around to see my grandkids."

Another shadow crossed her face and was gone. "Is Cassie thinking about having kids?"

Amy's familiarity with Cassie warmed him. He must've really talked his daughter up. "Someday. I don't expect to hear any news in the next couple of years, but she's almost thirty. I'm guessing it'll be soon."

"Hmm. I guess humans have a shorter window in their life when they're fertile."

He smiled. "Unlike cats and dogs."

Her brows shot up and she chuckled. "Right. It's not easy for all creatures to reproduce, but some don't have to worry about their biological clock counting down."

"And if she doesn't have kids, then she doesn't. I just want to be around if she does."

He expected another smile from her, but her brows drew together. "I wish you could be around for that, too."

"What about you, are your kids thinking about families yet?"

She finally smiled. "Not in the near future, either. Jace—Jason and...Megan...are enjoying their new marriages and their careers."

He grinned at the way Amy said "marriage" like it was a foreign term. He could relate. It was still hard to think of his little girl getting married and maybe having babies.

He stroked Amy's silky, warm skin. "What kind of grandparent do you think you'll be?" Why was he talking about grandkids? He was usually afraid of scaring away his dates because of his age. Not everyone was comfortable aging and dating men older than them, if only by a few years.

"Present, I hope," Amy said. "That sounded odd. Um...my kids and I are close, but we're also not."

"It's like they keep a part of themselves from you."

"Yeah."

They fell quiet and eventually, Gray drifted off. A black wolf with ethereal blue eyes haunted his dreams. They ran through the woods together and fear dogged their footsteps. He woke to Amy climbing over him, but she dropped a kiss on his head. "I'll call you later. Get some rest."

He was rolling off the couch when she finished dressing and was out the door. Gathering his clothes, he tried not to ponder her abrupt departure. One look at the time and he understood. It was after midnight and he had to work the next morning. Maybe she was just being considerate.

Did you think she wouldn't move on?

He brushed off the voice and went upstairs to bed. She said she'd call. And if she didn't, well, he would.

Rubbing his temples, he sat on his bed. Those weird dreams. He might have to choose paths through town for the next few weeks.

* * *

ARMANA PURSED her lips at her phone as she relaxed in her room after a sweaty run through the woods. The missed call from Gray taunted her. It'd been over a week since the night she'd irresponsibly hooked up with him. She knew better.

Sleeping with him was bad enough but getting to know him was worse. He was funny, relaxed, and attuned to her. She really enjoyed being with him—with or without clothing.

She toed her shoes off and sighed. They hit the floor with a clatter and she didn't move to pick them up. Earlier that morning, she'd run her wolf. During the afternoon, she'd applied for jobs, and God, that had made her feel oddly worthless. Begging to be of service somewhere. She caught on fast and training was always a breeze. Properly cordial and professional, she ticked all the boxes for any prospective employer, yet she had to go through the process. Interview, reference check, wait. Maybe they'd hire her, or they'd go with the applicant a fraction of her age with a raindrop of experience.

She paused to listen for anyone outside her room. Her door was shut, but shifter hearing might be keen enough to overhear the message Gray had left.

She hit play. "Hey, Amy." Argh, she hated when he called her that. "I'd like to see you again. We could have dinner this time or even go for a run. Either way, thanks for the other night." There was a small disgruntled sound before the voice-mail clicked off, like he was frustrated with his message but it was too late to take it back.

He was...adorable. Handsome. Virile. And a great cuddler. He made her feel seen. She hadn't connected her restless feeling at the lodge with the way she felt invisible living here. She hadn't adopted the Guardians as her pack, neither had she returned to Lobo Springs where her original pack lived. She wasn't a rogue, technically, but her stay here was only supposed to be temporary.

Yet, months later, here she was.

She didn't want to leave the Freemont area, but she didn't want to commit to a pack that saw her as a charity case.

She went back into her phone and deleted the message. Jace finding out about her and Gray at this pivotal time in her life would get her kicked out on her ass. No pack and not following the orders of the one who provided shelter for her wouldn't turn out well.

She'd just set her phone on the nightstand when footsteps resonated outside the door. Two sets. Male.

There was a tap on her door. "Mother."

Good. She was Mother today. Sitting up, she called, "Come in."

Jace entered with Commander Fitzsimmons. The two males filled her small space, highlighting what a small existence she'd pared herself down to.

"Is something wrong?" she asked. She breathed evenly, shoving a spike of anxiety down that they'd discovered she'd been with Gray. Like she was hiding a bad habit from her parents, she'd driven around for an hour with all her windows open to dilute Gray's scent. Then, like a spouse hiding a lover, she'd showered as soon as she arrived home.

Jace answered, his expression grim. "I've caught the trail of a trafficking syndicate that's even bigger than the one from last month. They're connected." He glanced at the commander, whose expression was as stone-faced as her son's.

The commander folded his arms. "Have you secured a job yet?"

His tone wasn't admonishing, not that it would be. He had his pack and all the trainees to worry about.

"No. I applied at several places today, but with college kids moving back for the school year soon, my options might be decreased."

He ducked his head. "That can work in our favor. We need all our people on this, but we also need to protect our loved ones."

"Can you stay with Cassie when she needs to go to town?" Jace asked.

"Of course." Armana licked her lips, debating her next question. It was one she would've asked, even before last week, or last month. "What about Gray?"

Jace's eyes darkened. "We discussed him. We can't take the chance of telling him about our world, then concealing it again."

She agreed. But Watching Cassie may get tricky when she wanted to visit her father.

"Cassie will keep in contact," Jace continued. "And hopefully, if he attracts the attention of the new rogues I'm after, we'll intervene in time. Gray's smart. He'll tell Cassie if he senses something off."

Only Armana had barely made it there in time. She hated the thought of putting him through emotional turmoil again, thinking he was relapsing. Just like he probably thought she wasn't calling him because he'd shared his schizophrenia.

She pushed the thought away and looked at Jace. "Are you leaving again?"

"In the morning. I don't know how long I'll be gone. We need to get these guys before they disband and disappear into the wind."

"And reassemble as soon as we let our guard down," Commander Fitzsimmons added.

"Tell Cassie I'll gladly be glued to her hip when she's in town, or be the shadow she doesn't see."

"Thank you." The heartfelt words from Jace threatened to choke her up.

"Always," she said. "Go enjoy a night of peace with your mate. I'm going to run to town."

She'd said the words before she'd committed to the thought. But as soon as the guys left, she had the phone in her hand messaging Gray.

Can I stop by?

CHAPTER 13

*T*his duty could drive her crazy. Armana sighed and did another scan around the office building Cassie worked in. Nothing unusual. The same couple was in deep discussion outside the door. Gestures were getting more exaggerated and punctuated. It might become a full-out brawl, though she tried not to wish it would escalate that far just to inject a shot of excitement into a monotonous day.

Some days, when Cassie was working, Armana would walk around the area. It was a business district. Office buildings, eateries, restaurants. She hated to stray too far, but she also had to balance her constant presence with not raising suspicion. If Cassie's coworkers saw her, Cassie would say that her car was in the shop and Armana was her ride. That took care of the time at drop-off and a good window around pickup, but the rest of the eight-hour shift, plus lunch, was harder to explain.

So she parked in various lots at different locations each day. Some days she walked in between switching up her parking job to another area. Other days she dressed in slacks and a crisp shirt and wore a no-nonsense expression like she was out and about on business. Her hairstyle varied depending on what she was wearing and she'd collected a variety of sunglasses to change up her appearance.

But it'd been three weeks of pretending. She'd identified shoplifters and people who stiffed their bill at restaurants by the way they exited the place. Rushing, looking behind them, smelling of guilt and the thrill of the crime. Three times, Armana had called in license plates to the cops.

That part had been fun. Figuring out each day was a sort of adventure. Then at night, she was free to roam and at least two nights a week, she landed in Gray's bed. When she was there, she did a perimeter sweep of his neighborhood, and at least once a week, she and Cassie drove by his work to check for shifters stalking him.

But the half hour waiting for Cassie to get off work was the worst time of her day. She sat here and thought about the massive amount of trouble she was building for herself. Falling for Gray had been too easy and she'd plummeted into his orbit. They talked about his work, her failure at finding a job even if she couldn't be truthful about turning down the interviews she did get. She loved the excuse, but it'd only make it harder to find places to apply to when the time came. She just couldn't commit when the timeline for nailing the trafficking ring was ambiguous at best.

Each interview she passed on should've frustrated her more, but relief was the only emotion that showed up. She could get used to this. Being useful to a pack during the day, involved in her son's life in a roundabout way, and a lover at home waiting for her.

She covered her mouth as a smile ghosted over her lips. It wouldn't do to have people see her spying on the mental health center and grinning to herself. Her license plate would be the next one called in. But she enjoyed the memory that had caused the good mood. She was going running with Gray this weekend.

Cassie wouldn't be going to town on a Saturday. Armana planned to meet Gray at a park by the river. He'd been complaining about the boredom of a ten miler and she'd offered her company. His reaction had been almost giddy.

Another smile threatened to make her look like she was ogling Cassie's work. Gray was so supportive, and he was always thrilled to learn something cool about her. Armana hadn't felt cool in a long time.

A widowed shifter could get used to his attention.

A widowed shifter had.

Her inclination to smile died a tragic death. What was she going to do? She'd have to break up with him. As soon as he was 100 percent safe. It'd be devastating.

She'd only survived Bane's and Keve's deaths because she'd had two kids to keep alive. Losing Gray unsettled her mind in too familiar a way. She'd have to put space between them while staying a distant part of his life through Cassie.

Sweet Mother Earth, that was going to suck. But she'd have to do it.

Cassie exited the employee entrance on the side of the building. She was on the phone, dammit. Cassie knew better than to let her phone distract her when walking through a parking lot. It must be Gray. Cassie caught her eye and the apology in them confirmed Armana's suspicion. They couldn't make Gray think anything was wrong, so Cassie had to answer his call like normal and she couldn't wait in the clinic while talking to him or Armana would've worried and gone in after her.

Cassie opened the door, still chatting with her dad. "It'll probably just be me. Jace might have to work but let me check with him before I let you know. 'Kay? Okay, I'll shoot you a text to let you know." She hung up and shifted in her seat so they could talk. "He wants me to come over for dinner Saturday or Sunday."

This was bound to happen. Gray had just mentioned the last time they were together that he hadn't seen Cassie in a while.

"You go, but drop me off a few blocks away. I'll get another walk in while you two visit."

"Are you sure? It doesn't seem fair."

Armana shrugged. "We can't meet, because explaining that I'm Jace's mom would be hard enough. I might not get a gray hair for another century. He'll notice I'm not aging like normal way before he wonders about you."

A shadow crossed Cassie's expression. "I have strong feelings about the Synod taking his memory. What dad is going to have issues with their daughter living a long, happy life?"

One who'd also worry about that daughter being in danger because she lived among shifters. But Cassie was correct. "Well, figuring out how to break away from your dad isn't an issue this weekend"—she gave Cassie a pointed look —"or even this year. So meet with him, have a good visit, and I'll keep watch and remain unseen."

Cassie broke into a smile and leaned forward to throw her arms around Armana.

Wha— Cassie had never hugged her before. She wasn't outwardly affectionate.

Armana patted her back and returned the embrace.

"Thank you." Cassie's voice was muffled. She pulled away. "I just… Times like this, when you talk rationally and I'm such a mess inside, make me feel like I have a mother again. I know things have been tense, but since you came back into Jace's life, I've always had you."

Armana couldn't speak around her astonishment. Cassie never failed to show her appreciation, but this was different.

"Anyway. I know I said thank you, but I mean it. Not just

for helping my dad or helping me, but for being there. Jace will come around. He *is* coming around, he's just guarded."

"I understand." Guilt flushed through Armana from head to toe. Regardless of her feelings for Gray, she'd be there for her kids and Cassie. She *was* here for Cassie. But would Cassie feel that way if she found out about the relationship with her father?

Jace wouldn't. He'd been waiting for his mother to abandon him again. He was an adult, but that didn't stop the emotions, the conflict, or the walls he'd built for himself against her.

She was going to have to breakup with Gray.

* * *

GRAY SELECTED his favorite shoes out of the lineup in his closet. He had a ten miler today and it was all about comfort. And looking good. Amy was joining him and with all the sweat a long run promised, he could at least look sharp.

His phone rang.

He answered with a grin. "Hey, Amy. Ready for ten?"

There was a long pause before she answered. "I'm sorry, Gray. I can't do this anymore."

His smile died. The gravity in her voice wasn't just about today. "What's going on?"

"I'm in a weird spot in my life and I'm not looking for anything long-term. It's not fair to you."

She was breaking up with him? They hadn't been seeing each other long, but it'd been hot, fiery, and it'd opened his life up to laughter and fun. He liked her. A lot. More than a lot.

"I understand," he said. He didn't. They were good together, not just physically, which was astounding, but they talked about everything from his mental condition to their lost spouses, their kids, feelings, hopes, aspirations. She made him feel young again.

"I'm sorry, that's all you need to understand. I'm really, really sorry we can't see each other. Goodbye." She whispered the last word.

The line went dead. That was all? He hadn't gotten to say...anything. *I guess there wasn't a need.* The finality had been in her words.

But it didn't make sense. They'd had long conversations, rounds of laughter, and long, blistering nights of sex. They'd been so hyped on each other they could barely make it through their greetings before they undressed each other.

Rubbing his chest, he set his phone down. He could wait a few days, then call or text, but his instincts said nothing would help. She'd made up her mind. End of discussion.

Staring at the shoes in his hand, the day lost its luster. A long run was planned and on the calendar. A long run was what he needed. Staying home to collapse into bed and replay the last month and what he'd done wrong and what he could've done better would only hurt him.

She was done with him.

Did you think she'd stick around forever?

Did you think she actually wanted you?

He stooped to slip his shoes on. His voices would shut up in the fresh air and physical exertion. He needed the voices to shut up.

Did you think you deserved her after you let your wife die?

Clenching his jaw and ignoring his bed where he'd spent many pleasurable hours with Amy, he went downstairs. He passed the couch without looking and collected his water bottle and gels.

He'd been looking forward to today for two weeks. His first run not alone. It'd been almost symbolic, like he was embarking on a life where he wouldn't be alone anymore, where someone fully accepted him.

She doesn't want you.

With a growl of frustration, he dumped his bottle and gels on the counter, toed off his shoes, and trudged to his living room. Grabbing his phone before his ass hit the couch cushions, he texted Cassie.

Can I get a rain check for tonight? Woke up not feeling well. Tomorrow night?

He shut his mind off and flopped on the couch. It was too early to order a pizza, but he found his phone and punched in an order.

No long run today after all.

GRAY GROANED HIMSELF AWAKE. Why did it feel like he had a twenty-pound stone in his gut? Between gut bombs of greasy pizza for lunch and dinner—and dessert—he'd watched nothing but reruns of old sitcoms. He blinked, his eyes burning against the bright light. Damn. He'd actually cried. Or maybe it was just the hours of gluing his eyes to the screen to keep from thinking about the long, lonely days ahead of him. He should be used to it.

Sitting up, he scrubbed his face. Empty pizza boxes littered the end table. A two-liter of soda sat next to the remains, two fingers worth left in the bottle. He'd finally fallen asleep and passed out on the couch.

He squinted at the time on his phone. Eight a.m. Could he take another day of self-pity?

Could he run ten fucking miles after consuming a vat of fat and carbs in the last twenty-four hours?

It'd hurt.

He was up for pain.

And he was getting his run in this weekend. He couldn't lose himself. His future unfolded in front of him. Another day of TV and pizza and he would go to work Monday depressed. The next run would get sloughed off and then he'd pass on the half marathon. Once his goals got ignored, his mental health got ignored.

Without bothering to change, he gathered his water—not bothering to refresh that either—and his gels. After a pit stop in the bathroom, he stomped out of the house and got into his car. At the park, he found a spot in the shade. A boiling car after a couple hours of running wouldn't be pleasant.

The first few miles of his run were slower than he'd planned as he purged himself—of the self-recrimination that he'd done wrong, not the pizza. The next few miles, he pushed his pace to outrun his anger at Amy for leaving him. He ran through the stages of grief, knowing it was only the beginning. He'd probably have to start over when he got home and was surrounded by memories and voices that knew how to hit his vulnerable spots.

But Cassie was coming over tonight. He had that to look forward to. Maybe he could even talk to her about it. He didn't usually discuss his dating life with his daughter, but he hadn't gotten as close to anyone as he had Amy.

The last two miles he slowed, barely above a walk. His legs ached, sweat beaded his brow, and he was tired in a good way. A shower would be welcome and an hour kicked back in his...not his bed. Somewhere he hadn't had sex with Amy.

That pretty much left the kitchen table. He couldn't go home without a self-care plan to get through the heartbreak. Maybe he'd catch a movie—at the theater. He couldn't do another night prone on the sofa.

Footsteps pounded behind him.

"My gosh, I didn't think I'd catch up with you," a woman said.

He glanced back. A woman approached, her ponytail bobbing with each step, her fitted athletic wear complementing her toned body. The midday sun gleamed off her blond hair, streaking it with gold.

She was attractive.

Geez, he had shitty luck. The last thing he wanted to do right now was chat up a woman, or anyone.

"Yeah, I'm almost done," he puffed.

She caught up with him and fell in step beside him. A move that only reminded him of when he'd run up on Amy. "I saw you flying by earlier. Nice form."

Flying by? Did she mean staggering and holding his gut?

He glanced at her. Her cheeks were flushed and she was breathing heavier than a walker would be. Had she been out running as long as him? It was almost noon. If she was running that long, shouldn't she be sweating? Or at least have a water bottle.

Enough with the conspiracy thinking. Not everyone was out to get him, and being on the receiving end of a woman's attention wasn't that unusual, no matter what his voices said.

"Thanks." He didn't know what else to say.

"Do you run here often?"

So she wanted to keep talking. He might as well. It's not like he was seeing anyone.

She's not interested in you.

Same old. "Sometimes. I like to change it up. You?"

"Oh, I'm kind of new to running. I dug out these old clothes and decided to try it again. I should probably get better shoes and something to carry a drink in."

The salesman side of him kicked in. "I work at the Sporting Warehouse and they carry a nice assortment of running gear."

She turned a mega-watt grin on him that would've made

his heart stumble any other day. "I'll stop in and check it out. Thanks."

They were approaching the park and the end of his long run.

He slowed to a walk. "Time for my cool down. It was nice meeting you." There. That wasn't exactly a brush-off, but he'd just had his heart broken and wasn't looking to kindle a flame with a stranger who could also break his heart.

She didn't keep running but walked next to him and stuck her hand out. "We didn't officially meet. I'm Jenna."

"Gray." He shook her hand to be polite, but he kept moving forward, not stopping to chat. It was critical to cool down properly, but why'd he feel guilty talking to another woman the day he got dumped?

"That's a cool name."

They reached the parking lot and he planned to stroll a few laps before his final round of stretching.

She broke off, shooting him another smile. How old was she? She looked younger than Amy. Did Jenna think him old enough to be considered safe to talk to?

Of course she's not interested in you.

Tossing him a wave, she trotted to a maroon hybrid. "Thanks for the info about the Sporting Warehouse. I think this running thing could become a habit. I'll have to stop in."

He returned the wave and tried not to stare as she drove off. For once, his insulting voices had been right. She wasn't interested in him, either.

He'd had his shot at love and lost it when Lillian died. When would he understand that it wasn't a good idea to fall for anyone else?

Too late. Amy had pulled the curtain back to reveal what loving and spending his life with someone could be like. Then she'd yanked the drapes back in place and he was left alone in the dark world.

CHAPTER 14

*G*ray's break was over, but before heading back to the floor, he stayed in the break room and checked his phone. A dangerous habit he'd developed over the last week.

No messages. Amy was truly done with him. He'd kept his word to himself and hadn't called or messaged her. He wanted to, wanted one more reason why they couldn't be together.

Then he'd curse himself for being naïve and needy. They'd dated for a month. Who got so obsessed they couldn't handle a breakup after a month?

But he missed her. Her laughter echoed through his house and the memory either chased his voices away or incited self-recriminations about how silly he'd been to think someone like her would want to build a life with him.

He shoved his phone in his pocket and strode out of the break room. Four more hours before the weekend started. His congenial mask was back in place. He liked working with people, needed it to avoid becoming a recluse who trusted no one. Some days were harder than others, and since he was more fatigued from training for his race this weekend, the voices bothered him at work when he had to deal with people. Sometimes the sensation of being watched niggled at him. If that happened, he took a bathroom break for some breathing exercises.

He would not regress over a breakup. The disappointment in himself would hinder any recovery. Losing his wife was one thing. Losing Amy shouldn't do more than make him disappointed for a week. Shouldn't, but it had. He'd lost sleep over it.

When he'd talked to Cassie about it, he thought he'd worked through his feelings. She'd supported his insight and had seemed grateful to have something to talk about with him.

She's not telling you everything.

No. She hadn't. The weariness in her eyes couldn't be hidden and when he'd asked what was wrong, she only said that Jace was having trouble at work and she worried about him. Cassie was meeting him for dinner tonight. She'd said Jace was gone more than usual, and paired with the extra stress, Gray wanted to be around for her. It was good to get himself out of his own mind.

"Hey, you."

He spun toward the familiar voice. Jenna was posed in front of a water bottle display, her hands on her hips and her chest pushed out. She wore navy-blue linen shorts that had a partial wrap around them, like they wanted to be a skirt but couldn't decide. Her striped white-and-lime tank top revealed toned and tanned arms. Her hair was down and without the sunlight, it was a darker blond.

When she smiled, the fine lines around her eyes were visible. She was older than he'd initially thought, putting her closer to forty and making him wonder again why she'd picked him out of all the runners on the path to chat up.

"Jenna," he greeted. His heart sank and all he could think about was this wasn't the woman he wanted to talk to. His work persona kicked in. "Are you finding what you need?"

"Yes and no. I thought getting a water bottle would be simple, but…" She gestured at the display that held at least twenty different kinds of bottles, all different shapes and colors.

He chuckled. "Well, let's start with plastic, glass, or steel?"

"Glass seems a little dangerous to run with."

He ran through her options for a good running bottle based on how she wanted to carry it and how long she planned to run. She chewed her lip and bent to check out the lowest shelf. The move shifted her skirt higher. Her bronzed thighs were toned and shapely.

Averting his gaze, he sidled over a few feet. He didn't feel like ogling anyone, and he was working and needed to be professional. Standing behind a woman with her ass sticking out wasn't a smart decision. He liked his job. It paid the bills, got him out of the house, and was predictable enough that he didn't go home frustrated. But there was enough variety that he wasn't caught in a Groundhog Day loop.

She rose and her gaze drifted over him. "This one is good."

Was she being suggestive? "Nice choice." He didn't look to see which one she'd picked. "Can I help you find anything else?"

"Shoes. Does it make me a bad runner that I'm not looking forward to buying shoes?" She smiled and looked up at him through her lashes.

"Not at all." He had the urge to scurry away. "I'll walk you there, but I don't work in women's shoes, so I can't help you."

"I bet you know a lot, though. You seem like a hardcore runner." Another smile. "You look like one, too."

He blinked at the odd compliment. He was fifty. He ran.

But stand him next to a collegiate athlete and he'd look like, well, a fifty-year-old.

"I use it to keep in shape. It's enjoyable of course, but it's easier than finding a biking path or worrying about flats when I'm ten miles out of town. You know, things like that."

They wove through the departments on their way to shoes.

"I'm thinking of hitting the trails this weekend," Jenna said. "Maybe we could meet up again? I could use the pep talk."

He flashed her an apologetic smile. Two months ago, he would've considered her invite, but this weekend he craved the solitude. And since he'd played the "I'm fine" game all week, he was going to reward himself with a peaceful run.

"I'm sorry, it's my last training run before the half marathon next weekend."

Her eyes widened. "You're doing the Freemont half? That race is like a party weekend in town."

He laughed. "Yes. Next year, I might do the full marathon, but I didn't decide in time to train for that."

"Still, that's how far?"

"A little over thirteen miles."

She whistled. "Nice. I might have to see what it's like. What time does it start?"

She wasn't thinking about meeting up with him, was she? Sure, he'd approached Amy all sweaty, but he hadn't expected what had grown between them. The marathon was his day. And Cassie was coming to cheer him on. She was an adult, but he never let his dates meet her unless it was serious. And none had gotten that serious. Only Amy had been serious and that relationship had ended almost as soon as it started.

Cassie would've liked Amy.

"It's early," he replied. "The gun goes off at seven for the marathon, then we're a half an hour later. My daughter is dropping by to be my support crew."

Jenna's brows popped and her smile faltered. "Your daughter? She'll be there?"

"The whole time. She's taking me out for brunch afterward."

A wide grin spread across Jenna's face. "Perfect." They reached the shoe department, but Jenna didn't make a beeline for the shoes. "Oh, I didn't realize the time. I need to get back to work. Maybe I'll *run* across you again."

She continued walking toward the exit. Her pun was cute, but he was wrapping his head around her sudden departure. Had he scared her off with talk of his adult daughter?

His interest in Jenna had been low to nonexistent, but it was the sharp edge that cut away to show how lightning had struck with Amy. He really missed her.

He sighed, rubbing his chest, and started back for the camping department he worked in. A few more hours and he could chat with Cassie about this weird encounter and how it unsettled him.

* * *

THE DAY WAS OBNOXIOUSLY bright and the birds were almost arrogant in their singing. As if Armana wanted to listen to them shout their mating calls all over the place when she'd just woken from sleeping alone, again.

She pinched the bridge of her nose as she waited inside Cassie's car in front of the lodge for Cassie to meet her. Her mental attitude had deteriorated harshly since she'd made that dreadful call to Gray. She'd tossed and turned each night for the past two weeks, only to catch a few winks before dawn when all the trainees started moving around. The commotion made it impossible to rest.

She needed her own place. It didn't help that when she envisioned a place in town, she pictured Gray's two-story house with its narrow staircase, worn carpet, and appliances as old as Cassie.

She heard Cassie's bounding footsteps and glanced up. Armana pulled herself together and forced a smile.

Cassie opened the door and collapsed in the seat. Had she run from her cabin all the way here? The way she was breathing, she must've sprinted.

Cassie grinned. "I didn't want to feel like a slacker when I'm going to watch my dad run thirteen miles. Crazy."

A sense of loss punched Armana in the gut. Cassie talked about Gray a lot and each time she brought him up, it was the same reaction.

"You must be proud." Armana pulled away, grateful today's bodyguard duties were going to be vastly different than sitting outside an office building, but she was dreading the risk of exposure and worse—seeing Gray all fit and triumphant and moving on without her.

"Totally. He even turned down a date because I'm going to be there."

Armana jerked the wheel. A date?

Cassie's hands flew to the dashboard. "Whoa."

"Squirrel," Armana said calmly, but her fangs throbbed. Visions of stalking a faceless woman filled her head. "You said your father's dating again?" Cassie had mentioned that Gray was reeling over a woman who'd broken things off. That conversation had been hard enough. Satisfying that her suffering from the breakup wasn't one-sided, but hard.

Yet two weeks and he was already diving back into the dating slurry?

Armana ran her tongue along a fang. She forced a calm facade when she really wanted to stop the car and shred its interior with her claws.

"Not really. There's this lady who's been in the store and was hitting on him. She sounded like she wanted to meet with him at the marathon, but he said he was spending the morning with me. Kinda sweet of him."

Armana's nostrils flared as her anger shifted from Gray to the unknown woman. Of course she'd hit on Gray. He was a catch. He was handsome, caring, funny, active…

And it was none of Armana's business. Tears prodded the backs of her eyes, but she refused to let them well up. Cassie would notice.

"He's a considerate man."

Cassie nodded and glanced over. "Is everything okay?"

Damn. She was too astute. "Tired. I haven't been sleeping well lately."

"Me either. Dad said he's been struggling, too."

Don't ask. Don't ask. "Is it from that breakup?" Well, she'd tried.

"He didn't say, but I think so. He and Amy didn't date long, but the way they clicked made him hope for more."

For the billionth time, Armana castigated herself for not walking away from Gray. Look what she'd done to both of them.

It was too late to worry about it now.

Armana threw her concentration into the drive to the rally point. She parked as far away in the parking lot as she could. Cassie planned to hop in with Gray and go grab some food. Armana would follow them in the car and rush back to the park when Cassie texted her they were leaving the restaurant. Then Gray would drive back and drop Cassie off while Armana hid in the trees surrounding the park. It was a convoluted solution, but this was an unusual scenario.

Cassie ran through the plan one more time before getting out. Armana watched her trot away, her heart sinking that she was so close to Gray and couldn't even say hi. Not that he would want to after she'd broken up with him—over the phone. She'd owed him more, but she'd doubted she could've gone through with it.

How did humans do it? Shifters moved from partner to partner, rarely forming attachments until they met their mate. This hookup and breakup stuff sucked.

A faint shot rang through the air. Armana glanced at the clock. That was the starting gun for the marathoners.

She scanned the crowd, searched the trees, and a half hour later the second shot went off. Gray would be running.

Several minutes later, Cassie arrived to hang out.

She crawled back in the passenger seat. "He said it'd take him a little over an hour and a half, so I'll go back to the start line in an hour to make sure I don't miss him."

A million questions ran through Armana's head and they all had to do with Gray. How was he doing? Had he slept last night? Was the woman who hit on him around? When did he think he'd start dating again?

Cassie's phone rang and she answered. Armana picked up Jace's low tone but couldn't catch the words. He spoke so only Cassie could hear him.

When she hung up, she had a wide grin. "He says they're really close to the lead rogue who runs the trafficking ring."

"That's good news." Another one would spring up, but each victory set the rogues back more and saved lives, no matter if Jace and his team would be hunting more traffickers next month or next year. "They must be planning their attack soon."

Concern darkened Cassie's brown eyes. "That's the part I hate. I want it over and I want him home. I'm used to him being on the road, but this ring was really embedded into our society."

Armana could've smiled at Cassie's use of "our." She was

165

one of them and she embraced it. *My son has a good mate. My daughter is happy. I can't ask for more.*

The hour went by and Cassie got back out. Armana hated being left alone with her thoughts. Jace's safety was always a worry. Maggie's, too. But knowing he was actively seeking out the most dangerous of their kind, possibly in the next twenty-four hours… It was hard on a mother.

And she didn't have anyone to talk to about it.

Cassie texted her Gray's bib number and when he'd hit the last checkpoint of the race. He was about done. She kept an eye on the time so she could watch for them in the parking lot. A white work van cruised the lot, intermittently blocking her view.

Find a parking spot, asshole.

Runners were drifting into the lot and finding their cars, grouping up and chatting. It helped and hindered Armana's cause. She had more obstacles to search through, but they blocked her view from where she was sitting in Cassie's car.

Move, people.

Finally, she spotted them. Her belly clenched at the same time her heart constricted. Gray's smile was broad and Cassie was talking excitedly next to him. A heavy medal hung around his neck and he wore the same running clothes from when he'd found her on the jogging path.

She wanted to run out and greet him, throw her arms around his neck, and revel in the solidness of his body. But they were from two different worlds that weren't allowed to collide.

That damn van was swinging around to block her view. It stopped right in front of Gray and Cassie.

Armana frowned and sat forward. *Idiots.*

A group of people behind the van turned to frown where Gray and Cassie were.

Fucking move. Armana put her hand on the door handle. A sense of wrongness filled the car.

The van finally pulled away. Gray and Cassie were gone. The onlookers shrugged and resumed their chatting.

Had they been abducted in broad daylight? In a move so smooth it was barely noticeable?

This had been well planned.

Armana jerked the car into gear and pulled out. The van wasn't speeding away and drawing attention to themselves. Armana wouldn't, either. They'd never see her coming.

CHAPTER 15

*H*is stupid voices had been right. And his paranoia had been valid.

Yet, he hadn't suspected the side door of the white van that had stopped next to them would slide open. He'd seen Jenna first and before his mind could work out how the van and the woman were connected, he'd seen the gun.

Make a scene or a sound and one of you is going down. Which one is gonna be a surprise.

They were too close to make a run for it without getting shot. They got in and he hugged Cassie close to him. Jenna confiscated their phones and all of his running gear. They rocked back and forth as the van drove away, and Jenna pointed a solid black gun at them. It looked bulky and heavy in her feminine hand, but her hard eyes matched the sinister weapon.

Nothing made sense, but it all made sense at the same time. Jenna hadn't been interested in him. Was the scrawny guy driving her real boyfriend?

Since Gray wasn't worth kidnapping, he connected the coincidences. Jace was having problems at work and he was in security. Jenna had struck when Cassie was with him. Gray had even made it easy for her and told her exactly when and where Cassie would be today.

"Your mate is being a giant pain in the ass," Jenna sneered, leaning against the sliding door and glaring at his daughter.

Cassie tensed next to him. "You're…human?"

Jenna's lips stayed twisted. "A human losing a lot of money because your mate is ruining our shipments."

What exactly did Jace do? And what else would Jenna be besides human?

Cassie cocked her head. "You supply the people. Oh my God, no wonder…" She snapped her mouth shut.

"No wonder we've been so hard to find?" Jenna *tsked*. "Shifters are so damn arrogant. They think rogues are on the road to mindlessness. Do you think maybe they just get tired of hiding among inferior beings?"

Rogues and shifters. A trickle of recall floated through Gray's mind. It sounded ridiculous. What do the rogues shift?

"But *you're* human," Cassie said. "You think you're inferior?"

"Not for long. I deliver you and he'll mate me."

Cassie shook her head.

Gray followed what they said but didn't understand it. "What are you mating?"

Jenna blinked at him, then turned her stare on Cassie. "He doesn't know?"

Cassie glared in return. Gray didn't say anything.

The driver snorted. Jenna tossed her head back and laughed, enjoying the power of knowledge over him.

He'd think she was crazy, but Cassie followed her conversation and his daughter was the sanest person he knew.

Jenna wiggled the gun, making him flinch. "This is priceless. Do you think she just married some guy and is living the dream? Nope, get this: he turns into a *wolf.*"

Gray stared at Jenna. Cassie didn't say anything. He wanted to tell Jenna that was ridiculous but the words didn't bubble up.

Jenna flicked the muzzle of the gun toward Cassie. "She's going to outlive you by more than decades. Try centuries. Has she told you that yet?"

Cassie shook her head, but it lacked conviction. It was a sad *please don't keep talking* shake. Why wasn't she calling Jenna absurd?

Just chalk up what you see next as evidence of the new world we're going to tell you about.

He'd heard that before, only that sounded like Amy's voice and she'd never said those words to him.

Yet his mind begged to differ.

Where were his voices? When he was suffering a paranoid state, he saw shadows and his voices were loud and incessant. But Jenna was clear and Cassie was real next to him.

He scanned the inside of the van. It was empty; the only seats were the driver's and passenger's. Gray couldn't guess what it'd been used for before, but the smell was definitely bleach.

They obviously had no issues with kidnapping. Had they killed in here before?

"What are you going to do with us?" Cassie asked. She didn't cower and her voice didn't shake. He was glad she wasn't alone, but he wished they'd just taken him instead.

"It's really too bad they sent your mate after my guy. A human mate with living family—it makes your dad a target and you and your shifter can't communicate telepathically." Jenna leaned forward and hissed, "He doesn't even know you're in danger."

Again, Cassie didn't refute Jenna's claims. Was she calling on her professional training?

That had to be it. People weren't telepathic.

Jenna waved the gun again. She was either a hand talker or liked how unsettling the motion was for her prey. "He will know when he tries to swarm my guy's compound. Only a picture of you two tied up will be waiting. If the Guardians attempt another assault..." She swung the muzzle toward Gray and made a shooting sound.

Cassie flinched.

Jenna switched her aim to Cassie. "They keep trying..." Her smile was cruel.

"I'm still unclear," Cassie said like her life hadn't just been threatened. "You think that the Guardians will leave you be because you've abducted me and my dad?"

"As long as they leave us alone long enough for me to gain my immortality."

"You'll be stuck with a mate forever that you may not like." Thatta girl. Play along with Jenna's delusions and make her second-guess herself.

"I don't care. I'll have money and I'll have health."

"I get the health, but where does the money come from?" Cassie asked.

Gray kept from looking bewildered. Immortality. Mates. Nonsense. But a part of him fluttered and he waited for a flood of information, anything. Nothing.

"I'm not quitting my job. Human trade is lucrative. And when we—"

"Jenna," the driver snapped.

Jenna's smug expression faltered, but she recovered. "Let's just say, there's room for growth."

The van rocked as they hit rough spots and potholes. Where were they going?

Gray couldn't see much more than sky over the front

seats. The sky and now trees, but they weren't close together. They were still within city limits.

He and Cassie swayed as the driver made several more turns. Jenna braced herself against the van door. Gray wished he were telekinetic and could open the door and dump Jenna on her ass with a wicked case of road rash.

They finally stopped. The driver got out and Jenna kept her gun trained on them. All Gray could see out the windshield was a large square warehouse painted a yellow that reminded him of baby vomit.

The driver got back in and pulled ahead. Darkness encompassed them and it was hard to make out the steel rafters and support beams.

Jenna flipped the handle on the side door and slid it open. She stepped out backward and kept her gun up. "Don't piss Tony off. He has an itchy trigger finger and"—she leaned forward and pinned Cassie with a nasty smirk—"he likes to sample the goods."

Over my dead body. And that was exactly how it'd turn out if Tony lifted a finger toward Cassie.

"Get out," Jenna barked.

He went first, keeping himself between Cassie and Jenna. The plan failed when Tony fell in step behind them.

Two metal chairs had been placed side by side in the empty stall next to the van. And like the van, the warehouse smelled like it had been doused in bleach.

Human trade is lucrative.

They were traffickers. Were they the ones Jace was after?

Gray frowned. Jace did security and Gray knew nothing about his work. But it made more sense than anything he'd heard tonight, and it'd explain why Jace was secretive about his work. Maybe he was an undercover officer.

Gray and Cassie were herded toward the chairs.

"Sit," Jenna ordered. "Tony's going to tie you up."

Both of them had guns. He and Cassie were unarmed and when his adrenaline wore off, he might collapse after the race and the kidnapping.

Tony made quick work of binding them with zip ties and duct tape to the chair with their hands behind their backs. Gray's legs were going to lose feeling from the constriction, then he'd stiffen up so badly that once he tried to move he'd fall on his face.

Jenna circled them and studied the work. "All righty. You two wait here."

She walked off with Tony. They went to a cramped office stuffed into the corner of the warehouse. The square window on one wall showed Tony dropping into an office chair and Jenna propping her feet on a desk with a phone to her ear.

"I'm sorry, Dad," Cassie said. "There's a lot about my life with Jace that I couldn't tell you."

"I'm sorry, too. Jenna's the one that was hitting on me."

Cassie's eyes flared. "That's how they did it. They used a human to watch you so they wouldn't be sensed."

A chill snaked down his spine. "Cassie, you're talking as senseless as Jenna."

She sighed. "No, I'm not. And I could explain everything, but until you see it with your own eyes, I'm afraid you'll only question your own sanity."

He was questioning more than his sanity, but not Cassie's. "Try me."

"First, I'll start with this: you knew everything and accepted it, but they had to wipe your mind."

"Come again?" He couldn't ignore the thrill of hearing that Cassie had trusted him with…whatever she was going to say…at one time.

"Jace, the people I live with, they're all shifters." As the story spilled from her, he waited for the moment he had heard enough fantasy.

It didn't come. It was oddly…familiar. The part he kept getting hooked on was Jace's mom, Armana. Each time her name was mentioned, a spike of intense interest speared him.

Cassie's shoulders dropped and her head hung. "So there it is. How are you doing?"

"I…don't know."

Cassie glanced at him. Her eyes narrowed. "You remember, don't you?"

"God, no. What you're saying is insane. What's bothering me is that I'm not sitting here telling you how crazy it is."

Her lips quirked. "They can't actually steal memories, they can only bury them. But I think your mind is stronger than we thought."

We. He couldn't blame her for thinking he was mentally fragile. Hell, twenty years ago he might've dissolved into a full breakdown, but all those exercises and self-care had really worked.

"Tell Dr. Sodhi that." Now wasn't the time for jokes, but the dad in him had to lighten the mood where he could.

"He'd agree." She stared at the office where Jenna danced to music that didn't breach the walls and Tony skimmed through his phone. "Jace said he was close to catching the leader. They must've set another trap."

There was nothing they could do. They were bound with no way to communicate and sequestered in an industrial park on a weekend. No one was around to hear their calls for help.

They had no choice but to sit and wait.

CHAPTER 16

*A*rmana had no choice but to make a move. "I have to go in, Commander. Once these two idiots find out that the trap failed, they're going to take it out on Cassie and Gray."

Her heart pounded. She'd been able to follow the van without being detected until they entered the industrial park. There was little traffic on a Saturday and her car would stand out like a beacon.

She'd ditched the vehicle and grabbed only her phone. Chasing the van had been easy; staying concealed hadn't.

She had called and briefed the commander as soon as she pulled out of the marathon parking lot, and he'd stayed on the phone ever since. He'd guessed that Cassie and Gray had been taken to keep Jace from killing the rogue in charge. Jace had known about the decoy location and was launching his assault as she stood by a storage unit and surveilled the warehouse Gray and Cassie were in. If only she had X-ray vision.

"Go," the commander said. "Jace's raid will be over soon and the kidnappers will either find out about the fail or get twitchy with their hostages. But Armana, I'm on my way. If there's too many for you to handle—"

"I won't endanger them with my stupidity."

"Keep your phone on you. If Jace's mission goes south all of a sudden, I might not be close enough to mind-speak."

"Got it."

Armana clicked her phone off and stuffed it in her pocket. She slunk around the storage unit and eyed the warehouse's security cameras. They faced the door obviously, but the sides of the building were clear.

The warehouse twenty feet away wasn't hooked up like this one. She angled away from her target and aimed for the neighboring building.

When she got close, she tracked the perimeter, keeping clear of the other warehouse's security. There wasn't a good way to the roof. She tried the next building over.

It had a second level and a fire escape. Perfect.

She scaled the rickety stairs and hauled herself to the roof. Running across it, she picked up speed and leaped to the next roof.

One more jump. Thank the Mother she was wearing athletic shoes. She took the jump, clearing the expanse between roofs. As lightly as she could, she landed and rolled to a stop. Listening carefully, she waited to hear if anyone inside panicked.

Nothing.

She crawled to a vent. It was too small to fit through, but she skirted around it to see inside as much as she could. The warehouse was a bare metal skeleton. They probably didn't care who suffered inside during the winter; they'd only built a structure to move product. In this case, people.

Another vent erupted from the edge of the roof. It was rectangular and she could shove herself through it.

But it was bolted on. She had no tools.

Well, she was strong and she healed quickly. She tugged and pried at the grate until her fingertips were raw and bleeding. When it was loose enough to give her wiggle room with the bolts, she worked her way through each one and set them aside to avoid the ruckus of tearing metal from metal. Lifting the vent, she went slow to keep the noise down. It screeched in her sensitive ears, but she scented only humans inside.

The vent opening was clear. She inhaled. Gray and Cassie and a male and female. Fresh exhaust, presumably from the van. Her nostrils burned from the strength of the bleach vapor. Under it all, she smelled terror, human sweat, tears, and other bodily fluids that made her own blood boil.

The supports provided her more than enough options to climb into the building. Nimbly, she lowered herself down.

Gray and Cassie came into view. They were next to each other, tied to their chairs. Neither of them appeared hurt. She scooted along a dusty beam. An old nest, a hazard of the big doors being left open too long, was wedged above her head and the feathers left behind tickled her senses.

She scrunched her mouth to each side and wrinkled her nose. As she was fighting not to sneeze, Gray glanced up and started.

"Amy?"

Cassie jerked her attention around and looked up. Then she stared at her dad. "Did you call her *Amy*?"

Armana put her finger to her lips. She wanted them to quit talking for more than one reason.

Cassie and Gray both snapped their attention to the floor in front of them, but Gray lifted his gaze back to the ceiling. Armana shrugged.

"Dad," Cassie hissed. They both looked to the corner.

Armana swung to another rafter to get a clear view.

Voices filtered out from a haphazard room. It had a frame and walls but only a tin roof across the top to give it some privacy from the rest of the place.

Another two rooms bordered one side and the stench of bad plumbing emanated from them. Bathrooms. She concentrated but didn't sense others besides the two humans she planned to kill.

Brilliant strategy, though, rogues working with humans. They'd probably lied, bribed, and promised all kinds of treasure to these two idiots. Rogues wouldn't keep their word. If they were capable of it, they would have stayed with their pack or started their own, not broken the laws of their people. And rogues knew they wouldn't be allowed to exist outside of a pack setting, so why not sign their death warrant and tell humans about their existence?

It was a mess, but that was what her son and Maggie dealt with. Armana needed to rescue Gray and Cassie, then face her own reckoning for interfering in Gray's life.

She evaluated the structure. The walls had been insulated, rendering them useless to climb down. She couldn't risk jumping straight down onto concrete. If she were outside on dirt or grass, that'd be different. In here, it was just her and her sore bare hands. She couldn't afford to twist an ankle.

There were four support beams. She could scale down one of them. Two were in the office window's direct line of sight. The other wasn't close to cover of any sort. She chose the one between the van and the far wall.

Darting along the rafter, she made her way across the warehouse, holding her arms out for balance and grabbing cross supports when she needed to jump across.

She glanced back to check the office. No one had come out, but the atmosphere had changed. What was different?

The music had quit playing.

Gray and Cassie tracked her the entire way, their gazes burning into her. Armana reached the support and used her hands and feet to scale down it. She'd reached halfway when a "What?" rang from the office.

The office door flew open. Cassie gasped. Armana dropped the last twelve feet and landed in a crouch.

The woman stormed out, her face twisted. So, they'd found out Jace hadn't fallen for the trap this time.

"How'd he know?" the woman shrieked.

The man emerged from the office and as he was turning in her direction, Armana scurried behind the van. She stayed low, keeping under the van's windows. The woman shouldn't see her if she was confronting Gray and Cassie.

"How did who know?" Cassie asked shrilly. "Did something happen to Jace?"

Armana swelled with pride. Cassie wasn't panicking, she was covering for Armana.

Footsteps approached.

"Tony?"

Armana tensed, hoping the woman wouldn't come looking for her partner.

Tony didn't respond. He was close. Armana lifted her gaze. Sure enough, the muzzle of the pistol cleared the back of the van first. But she didn't go after that. She spun around the bumper and aimed a fist into his groin. Moving too fast for him to react, she nailed him. He dropped with a cry and she snatched the gun from him.

"Tony?"

Armana fixed her grip on the weapon. The familiar weight brought back a lot of memories of her days before being a mom. She shot Tony in the head. His body went limp, and her ears protested the noise.

She stormed around the van. The woman's disbelief was satisfying, but Armana didn't waste time.

The woman swung her gun up, but Armana had already aimed.

Squeeze.

The first shot hit a shoulder. The woman blinked before a mask of pain covered her face.

Armana took the extra second to aim center mass. The woman jerked as a second hole ripped open in her shirt. She collapsed. Armana rushed to free Cassie.

Gray stared at the woman, his mouth hanging open.

Cassie's expression was filled with relief. "Oh my God, Armana. I was hoping you saw them take us."

"Armana?" That snapped Gray's attention back to her.

"This is Jace's mom. Are you remembering any of that?"

Armana's phone buzzed in her pocket, but she had to untie Cassie to work on Gray before she could answer the phone. Whoever that woman had talked to on *her* phone could be waiting for her to return with information.

"I know her as Amy," Gray said. He was craning his head around to watch her.

"I'm sorry, Gray," Armana muttered as she ripped through duct tape at Cassie's hand only to find zip ties underneath. She snapped them apart.

"As in the Amy you were…"

"We'll have to talk about this later." Armana couldn't look Cassie in the eye as she scooted around front to work on her feet. She paused to pull her phone out and toss it to Cassie.

Cassie was rubbing her wrists and fumbled the phone. She righted it. "It's Commander Fitzsimmons."

Armana finished Cassie's legs and moved to Gray.

"Cassie told me everything," he said.

"But you don't remember." She did his legs first. Freeing his hands from behind his back felt too much like hiding.

"Not really."

Good. He was holding up well.

"Cassie said you weren't supposed to contact me?" he asked.

Her mouth quirked. "You encountered me, if I remember correctly."

A faint smile touched his lips. "Yeah, I guess I did."

Cassie broke in. "The commander can't make it here in time. Jace got the leader of the ring, but the second-in-command is missing. They think he was the contact for Jenna."

"Who?" Armana saw where Cassie was looking. "Oh."

Gray's legs were done and he started stomping his feet and flexing his muscles to get blood moving. She went to his hands.

Cassie stood. "He said we need to get out of here. They'll be more intent on revenge than ever before."

"Find the keys to the van." Armana ripped and snapped until Gray's hands were free.

He stood slowly, wincing at his stiffness. The inactivity after his race was taking its toll.

Armana twined her arm through his and led him to the van, but he pulled her off course. Cassie was patting down Jenna. He circled the van.

"Tony was the driver," he said.

They riffled through Tony's clothing until Armana found the keys in his pants pocket.

She was about to call to Cassie when the sound of an engine broke through the quiet industrial park. Dammit, what were the chances it was some contractor going to a nearby warehouse do some paperwork on a Saturday?

The engine stopped in front of their warehouse.

"Get in the van," Armana ordered.

She pulled Gray with her around the van. He got inside

181

with Cassie and she let him shut the door as she ran around the front.

The overhead garage door flew open. Two burly males were in the opening, both holding rifles.

Shifters. She couldn't take two armed shifters. Armana dove into the driver's seat and fired up the engine.

The males opened fire. Flinging the gearshift into reverse, Armana stomped on the gas and turned the wheel to aim for the shifters.

The van shook as it was peppered with bullets. They sprayed the vehicle. Armana ducked as low as she could. Glass shattered. She grunted as one bullet ripped through the front seat into her.

She gritted her teeth against the searing pain. Nothing vital was hit. The shifters scattered and bullets quit flying. As soon as she was clear of the warehouse, she shoved the van into drive and floored it.

The wheels screeched and laid a black strip on the asphalt. Air whistled through the holes and broken windows.

Fire wicked up her side, but she'd only been hit once. Blood bloomed through the cab. It wasn't just hers. Sweet Mother Earth.

"Everyone all right?" She couldn't look behind her or she'd careen off the road at the speed she was going.

Cassie's voice was muffled. "Dad?" Pain filled that word. "Dad!"

Cold washed through Armana. Gray's blood stained the air.

"Gray?" She kept her eye on the rearview mirror as she watched the road. The shifters were in pursuit.

"Dad." Cassie grunted. Armana spared a look. It was worse than she'd feared.

Gray had covered Cassie. He'd had no idea. He was doing

what any loving father would do. He wouldn't know that Cassie's bond with Jace would heal her wounds.

"How bad?" Armana asked. She took a hard turn and Cassie cried out in pain.

"I'll be fine. One hit my thigh." Her voice was tight with agony. "Dad—he's—blood everywhere." A sob escaped.

Armana clenched her jaw. *Commander?*

Was she close enough to him yet?

"Do you have the phone, Cassie?"

"Um...I don't...I don't know." The normally calm and collected Cassie was barely hanging in there. "We need to get him to a hospital. His pulse is weak."

No. They couldn't. As soon as they slowed down, the shifters pursuing them would finish them off. They weren't concerned about raising suspicion about their kind and wouldn't hesitate to follow them into a hospital parking lot and hurt other innocents to get to them.

But would Doc have the capability to save him? He was stocked for a lot, but not for plain humans who might need life support. She had to try. Gray would have the protection of the Guardians.

"What injuries can you see, Cassie?" Armana swerved but didn't dare get too wild. It'd be hard on Gray and they could crash. *Commander?*

Dammit, he didn't answer, and Cassie was too busy with her dad. *Please be okay, Gray. I can't lose another person I love.* The thought came out of nowhere.

What's going on? the commander's voice filtered through her mind. Had he heard that?

Two males arrived and opened fire. Cassie and I are hit, and Gray is hurt and unconscious. I think he's bleeding out. We're in a white van heading toward the lodge. The shifters are in a dark blue SUV and they're going to get more aggressive the farther out of town we get.

I'm on the highway. When you see us, give it all the gas you can. We'll get between you and them.

Who was with him? *They have assault rifles.*

So do we. I'll tell Doc to expect you.

Good to know. "How's Gray?" She was going to ask Cassie that every minute.

"He's hardly breathing." Cassie sniffled. "I'm trying to stop the blood, but there's so much."

"We're almost there."

"Why aren't you going to the hospital?"

"Cassie—"

"Armana! I don't care about shifter politics."

Cassie's assumption that Armana was choosing politics over Gray stung. She didn't care about the logistical cleanup going to a human hospital would require; the Guardians would take care of any mess with the humans. It didn't help she was worrying she'd made the wrong decision.

"Cassie," she tried again. "I care about getting pulled over. Do you think a police chase, or worse, stopping to get pulled over and suffering a drive-by shooting, would help Gray? We need to get to Doc." A hospital would be the best thing for him, but it was also the quickest way to lose him.

The pursuers accelerated, attempting to creep up beside her, but Armana swerved enough to make it too difficult. Cassie was murmuring to Gray. Armana hated the shifters behind her for hurting Gray and for keeping her from being by his side.

This was the third time she'd been tossed into Gray's life and couldn't just be with him. That was all she wanted. What she did for a living, where her home was, she didn't care. With him, she was where she wanted to be. She hadn't had that kind of peace in her life in a long time.

Armana jerked the wheel to the right, harder than she

intended. The van careened down into the ditch. She eased it back up, the vehicle jumping and jostling.

"Stop!" Cassie pleaded. "I can't keep pressure on him if we're jumping around."

Hopelessness swelled. The work van couldn't win a race with a car and she hadn't spotted the commander. She couldn't seem to keep from hurting Gray, and she wasn't going to be able to save him.

CHAPTER 17

*A*rmana checked the mirrors. A car was coming. Not the commander. The two they'd already passed on the highway were the only things that had saved them from getting run off the road and crashing into a tree.

The shifters chasing them had a shred of self-preservation. A human calling the cops would hinder them as much as it'd risk Gray's life.

The car passed. The shifters hit the gas.

They were getting close to the turn-off point for the back roads to the lodge. That also meant the terrain got hillier and no amount of gas was going to make this wad of metal go faster.

The van got rammed.

Cassie cried out and Armana jerked forward. Gray wasn't going to survive if they kept doing that. The car was so close, the driver's steely gaze was clear in her rearview mirror.

So was the passenger opening the window to lean out with a rifle.

Sweet Mother Earth. She and Cassie could sustain more

bullet wounds, but Gray couldn't, and Cassie wouldn't be able to care for him.

She crested the hill. A black SUV flew toward them.

Armana let out an unexpected *whoop*.

Alex was hanging out of the back driver's window, a round metal cylinder on her shoulder. As soon as the commander cleared the van, the shifters swerved and careened into the ditch. A blast echoed, rattling the van like a giant soda can.

The car flipped when the round from the...whatever Alex was using hit it. Flames erupted from inside. If the shifters got out, Alex could pick them off. Or they'd go down with their ride. Either way, Armana didn't have to worry about them anymore.

The scene disappeared behind her. Armana kept going, but she couldn't breathe a sigh of relief. "How is he?"

"He's fading fast. There's so much blood."

Armana tightened her grip on the wheel. "Turning. Brace yourself."

She slowed as much as she dared. They hit the gravel and she increased the speed. Trees flew by and the road was empty. Within minutes, the lodge stretched before them, offering all the hope Armana could fantasize about.

Would Doc be able to work a miracle?

As if her thoughts conjured him, Doc strode out of an open garage door, pushing a cot draped with a white sheet.

Why white? So she could see Gray's life draining from him?

She didn't slam on the brakes but eased to a stop. Doc maneuvered the cart to the side door and shrugged off the jump bag he'd slung over his shoulder. Armana hopped out and ran to him. Doc had the door open and had crawled inside by the time she got there.

He kneeled at Gray's head and Cassie hadn't moved from

his side. Gray's skin fit his name. Ashen. And blood. So much blood a human couldn't spare.

Cassie's top was stained red and her leg was stuck out straight like it'd cramped that way. Streaks of Gray's blood on her face were smudged with tears, and her hair was shoved in all directions.

Armana met Cassie's watery gaze. The terror inside mingled with an acceptance that broke her heart.

"No." Armana's voice cracked. She lifted herself inside and inched to Gray's side.

Doc's heavy gaze was enough. "I'm sorry. He needs blood. All the saline in the world won't stabilize him."

Cassie grabbed Doc's arm. "C-can I give him mine?"

"Mine as well." Armana scooted closer. Her fingers found Gray's cool ones, sticky with his blood.

Doc's expression fell. "He can't heal like us. It'd leak out as fast as I could get it into him."

"There's got to be something we can do." Cassie's fingers dug into Doc's skin; he didn't flinch. "He can't die. I'm not ready for him to die."

Gray's fingers were limp. Armana squeezed them. Her own pain resonated with Cassie's.

He can't heal like us.

What if... What if Gray was one of them?

No. She couldn't.

But some widows and widowers had found another mate.

Gray was unconscious. He couldn't decide for himself. This didn't fall under a medical power of attorney.

"I could..." She tried to force herself to quit talking. Could she forgive herself if she didn't toss the idea out there? "I could mate with him."

Cassie's gaze pinned her. Doc's brows rose and he leaned back as if he wanted nothing to do with the decision.

Cassie blinked. "You'd do that?"

"More importantly, would he do that?" Armana waited. She couldn't make this choice alone. It was tampering with someone's life, how they lived it, *who* they lived it with. She and Gray would be connected until one of them died.

Biting her lip, Cassie spared a glance at her dad. "You're Amy."

An explanation hovered on Armana's tongue, but all she said was "Yeah."

"Do it."

"We need the *gladdus*," Doc said. He didn't argue, and his expression was resolved, as if he'd decided it wasn't his consequence to deal with and he wasn't going to hinder saving a life. "One of you needs to find one and one of you needs to stay and be a blood donor or he won't make the ceremony."

"I have one." Armana leaped out of the van.

She sprinted through the lodge to her room. Grabbing hers from on top of her dresser, she spun out of the room and ran back to Gray. As she cleared the garage she yelled, "Can you do the ceremony?"

Doc nodded, busy hooking his rigged tubing to a needle protruding from Cassie's arm. He unwrapped the other end and stuck the needle into Gray's neck. Red flooded the clear plastic.

Armana skidded into the van and slapped the dagger on the floor by Doc's knee. The four of them were crowded in the van. It'd be an intimate ceremony, with ramifications Armana couldn't stop to think about.

She lifted Gray's hand and looked at his face. His jaw was slack, his eyes closed. The dark lashes rimming his eyes were stark against his cheek. She couldn't stand to see him without his vitality and easy smile.

"Do it," she said, mimicking Cassie's earlier words.

Doc stumbled through the ceremony. When he got to

spots where he couldn't repeat the right phrase, Cassie filled him in. Armana shot her a small smile. Cassie had been the most recently mated out of all of them.

When it came time to clasp hands for the blood exchange, Doc inserted the blade between her palm and Gray's.

"Wait." Armana slipped her other hand around Gray's. She might be using the same dagger that had mated her and Bane, but she couldn't overwrite the mark left behind.

Doc nodded, his eyes full of understanding. He'd lost his mate, too. Armana inclined her head to let him know she was ready.

The cut was quick. A flash of pain, replaced by warmth spreading out from where their hands were connected.

"It's done," Doc said. He cleaned the blade and put it back into the box. Next, he disconnected Gray and Cassie. Blood would help speed healing, but Cassie had her own injuries to mend. Armana didn't move. Neither did Cassie.

Doc packed his things. "We need to transfer him to the infirmary. He has a long road ahead and it'd be better if he were clean and comfortable when he woke."

Woke to find his life irrevocably changed against his will. Armana stiffened.

Cassie wiped her face. "Yeah. I guess we'll have some explaining to do."

Armana blew out a heavy breath. There was a line of people to come clean to. "To more than just your dad."

She was mated. Again. As they dragged and lifted Gray to the cot, memories of her first mating ran through her mind.

It'd been spring. Not the end of summer. She'd been jubilant, conceited even. Nothing was going to destroy her happiness. She had mated a strong male that she was crazy about and they were going to rule together. The day had been all about her as she'd danced around the campfire and showed him off.

She brushed her fingers along Gray's salt and pepper hair as Doc wheeled him to the infirmary. From arrogance to shame. She'd claimed a man's life without his knowledge, and she still couldn't convince herself it'd been the right thing to do. Just like she couldn't bring herself to regret not letting his life slip away.

Would he be able to forgive her?

$* * *$

DULL, throbbing pain racked his body. Gray didn't open his eyes right away. Fatigue weighed on him like he'd run a half marathon a day for weeks.

He groaned and turned his head but kept his lids shut. Tentatively, he inhaled. His chest was tight, but his gut clenched. Had he done an ab workout he didn't remember?

The stiffness in his legs was to be expected. He had just finished a race—

His race. Images bombarded his mind. Cassie. Jenna. A van. Amy— Armana.

His eyes flew open. Amy was Armana.

He remembered Armana. Cassie had said his memories were bound.

Blinking against the dim overhead light, he tried to sit up.

That was a no-go. Warm hands gently pressed on his shoulders and the most delicious scent filled his nose. He glanced from the light to the person settling him back down.

"Armana."

She smiled, but it was tight. Her shoulders were tense, but her gaze was relieved. How did he notice all these details?

Like her pale eyes and how they darkened with any emotion other than happiness. Her fresh spring-breeze scent. Had she switched shampoos?

Armana was Amy. She'd dated him, then devastated him. Now he knew why. All the information was there.

They'd been trapped in the warehouse. That was the last he remembered.

"Those guys," he croaked.

"Dead," Armana answered. "You're in the lodge. You were shot four times."

He jerked up again, but Armana held him down. He was as weak as a toddler. Flopping on his back, he ignored the protest in his joints.

"We didn't expect you to wake this early." She turned from him, and he mourned the loss of her heat.

He frowned. He'd been stripped of his clothes. Where had he been shot? Must've been all over.

Water tinkled from the other side of her, though it was as if he had earbuds streaming the noise straight to his eardrums. The sound was crisp, just like her scent, but not nearly as pleasing.

Wait, if he'd been shot in the van— "Cassie? Was she hurt?"

Armana spun back to him, a wet rag clutched in her hands. Was she washing him? "She's healed already, and she's right outside with Jace. We have a lot to talk about."

There was shuffling outside the door. He reached down to make sure he was covered before the heavy metal door swung open.

Cassie rushed in first. Her smile was wide, but like Armana, the underlying tension couldn't be hidden. Jace and Commander Fitzsimmons filed in behind her.

"What's wrong?" He was concerned about his daughter. Anxiety radiated from her.

The commander crossed his arms and leaned against the stark white counter. He nodded to Armana. "You might as well explain it all while I'm here."

The commander reminded Gray of himself when Cassie was four. She'd unrolled an entire roll of toilet paper into the toilet and flushed. Then flushed again when it wouldn't go down. She'd run and Gray had stepped, literally, into the mess. He'd stood just like the commander when he'd demanded an explanation.

Potty-geddon had only inconvenienced an afternoon and their washing machine. What Armana and Cassie had to say was on another level. He didn't know how he knew that.

The room went silent. Cassie stared at Armana, her eyes wide. Armana wrung the cloth and drops splattered to the floor. A muscle jumped in Jace's jaw, but he stayed by Cassie's side. He was staring at his mother, but his expression was carefully measured to hide any emotion.

Cassie opened her mouth first, but Armana interrupted. "You called me Armana when you woke, so you have your memories back, yes?"

He nodded. His aches and pains had vanished, his curiosity too strong.

"That's to be expected," she muttered. "It only works on humans." Her gaze jerked to Jace. A muscle popped in his jaw. She met Gray's gaze again. "I mated you to save your life."

"Excuse me?" He'd heard every word. None of it made sense. He'd had that feeling a lot recently.

"You're still human, but you're not." Armana pressed her fingers to her temples. "I'm messing this up."

"Ya think?" Jace's eyes sparked icy fire. "Go back further and tell the commander what was going on."

Armana folded her hands together. Her gaze dropped to the floor. "We were seeing each other."

"But Dad found her," Cassie said. "She didn't—"

"She didn't walk away," Jace growled. Cassie snapped her

mouth shut and narrowed her gaze on Jace, displeasure rippling through her expression.

Gray had little clue what was going on, but they obviously knew she'd been going by Amy and continuing to see him. He would not let his drama come between his daughter and her...mate.

Armana had said she'd mated him. What exactly did she mean? That could wait until after he cleared up the issue for Jace.

He struggled into a sitting position. Armana was at his side, but she didn't stop him. She held her hands away as if she were afraid to touch him in front of the others.

"I dreamed of Armana." Her brows shot up at his confession. He wished he could pull her next to him. "I ran all over town like a madman." Probably not the best choice of word. "I was driven by some instinct. I found that cabin."

The cabin. Oh yes, he had all his memories. He cleared his throat and persuaded his brain to not dive into the memories or he'd be sporting an inappropriate erection.

"Oh my God." Jace stepped forward, but Cassie caught his arm. "You two were sneaking around even then. Armana, don't you think about anyone but yourself?"

"Don't talk to her like that." Gray had never heard himself speak like that. Low. Dangerous.

Jace's gaze flickered and he eased back. "Explain."

Armana's hand lifted and Gray grabbed it, twining his fingers through hers. She didn't look at him.

"Yes," she answered. "We were attracted to each other instantly, and we acted on it."

"But then I found her and asked her out." Gray smiled at her, coaxing a ghost of a grin from her. Was she remembering how he'd charged up on her like a maniac? "She turned me down."

"Then I didn't." She lifted a shoulder. "I couldn't stay

away. But eventually… I couldn't see a way it wouldn't end in disaster. So I broke it off." She squeezed his hand. "I didn't want to."

"Then Jenna started hitting on me." He told the rest of what he remembered. When he was done, he looked at Armana. This was the part he needed to know, but he didn't really care. His daughter was in the room, safe, and with her mate, who was also unharmed. And Armana was with him.

The rest was the small stuff.

Cassie jumped in. "He covered me when the shifters opened fire. I got hit, but"—her eyes brimmed—"he got hit." Jace hugged her to him.

"We couldn't go to the hospital without the shifters finishing the job and probably taking out me and Cassie, or calling attention to our kind." Guilt. He inhaled. It was like he could smell the emotion coming off of Armana. Was this a new symptom of his disease? She squared her shoulders and looked her son in the eye. "We made it here, but Doc couldn't help him. I mated him to save his life."

Mated. "Is that why I feel different?"

Cassie nodded. "Your senses will grow stronger over time, but you won't be like a natural-born shifter. And you won't have their abilities."

"But you'll share my life span," Armana said softly. "And I'll share yours. One of us goes, the other goes."

Because he was human. Sort of. He waited for the voices to tell him how she was lying and how she was trapped with him, and she was, but they were quiet. They couldn't gain ground beyond his astonishment.

"So, we're, like, married?" he asked. "Wait. I thought mates could tell they were supposed to be…you know, mates."

Commander Fitzsimmons broke his silence to explain. "Most wait until they sense their mate. There've also been

195

cases of shifters losing their mates and meeting another. But we can tempt fate and bond with whomever we want."

Even when they were unconscious, apparently. "Will this be a problem?"

The commander cocked a rusty eyebrow. "Depends. When you two were dating, did she reveal herself?"

"No," Gray said. He'd been happily ignorant.

Armana shook her head.

"Then what happens next is in your hands. Do I have to deal with a shifter who mated someone without their knowledge or their consent?"

"But she saved my life."

The commander shrugged. "I have to report to the Synod. You're going to tell me what to say. But…" He planted his hands on his hips, the move intent and intimidating. "You don't have to decide how violated you feel now. Take some time, think on it. Alone."

They all stared at him.

"With Armana," the commander clarified.

"What?" Jace sputtered.

Commander Fitzsimmons leveled him with a burning stare that'd drop a lesser male. "Because I don't want Cassie's 'thank god you're not dead' to influence his decision to spend his life with your mother. And I don't want you filling Gray's head with old resentments that are between you and your mom and not Gray and your mom. I'm not forcing Gray to spend a life with someone he doesn't want to; neither am I forcing it on your mother. Gray feels violated, he comes to me. Armana feels trapped, she comes to me." The hard gaze turned on Gray. "But ultimately, since this was forced on you, the final say is yours. Let me know what you decide."

He stalked out the door, opening it with a clang that made them all jump.

"I trusted you," Jace said to Armana. "I trusted you to take care of Cassie, and you…" He shook his head and stormed out.

"I'll talk to him." Cassie didn't leave right away. She crossed to him and threw her arms around his neck.

"It'll be all right, peanut."

Would it? Jace was angry at his mother. Gray had a new life to adjust to and he had the commander's words echoing in his head. *Armana feels trapped, she comes to me.*

EVENING HAD LONG since fallen by the time Armana and Gray reached his house. Unloading her luggage from her car, Armana dreaded the night to come. Gray had been quiet after the commander had made his decree. Jace and Cassie hadn't seen her off. Gray's car had still been at the marathon parking lot. Armana had given him a ride to his car, but he'd been lost in his thoughts all the way there.

That was one tense drive she'd rather not experience again. In his home, she'd be able to retreat somewhere, anywhere, if he continued his silent treatment.

How upset was he? She couldn't tell. A lot of things had to sink in for him and how they'd settle was a mystery.

She'd parked on the street and Gray had pulled into the garage, leaving it open behind him. She hefted her bag and followed in his wake, glad he was unlocking the house door.

"It seems like forever since I've been back," he said.

She was about to say, "Me, too," but that would only highlight how she'd given him a fake name, led him on, then broken up with him. So she swallowed the words and went inside.

The familiar smells of his house sank into her psyche. She liked how it always smelled like he'd just made a meal. A pleasant hazard of cooking at home so often. The air was laced with his shampoo and conditioner and aftershave, all simple department-store buys.

"Hungry?" he asked.

How could she be with the mess of emotions inside of her? She wasn't here to win him over. Her first reaction at the commander's orders had been a surprise. Either he wasn't worried that she'd seduce Gray with her wiles, or he didn't think she could, or he thought it'd solve enough problems if she did.

She wanted to seduce Gray, that was the problem. But she couldn't. He had to decide whether or not he could spend the rest of his forever with her.

"You need nutrition," she said. "Lots of red meat if you have it."

"I do, actually. I usually feast on chicken, but I'd planned to celebrate my race with a few steak nights."

She followed him from his garage through a small coatroom and into the kitchen. He went straight for the fridge and withdrew some steaks, along with bell peppers and onions and mushrooms. Was he going to make kabobs?

Her stomach rumbled. She had her own healing to do and hadn't eaten anything all day.

She caught herself staring at his back as he prepped their supper. Her main excuse was admiring the play of muscles across it, but mostly she didn't want to ask the next question.

"Where should I put my bag?"

He paused midslice and faced her. "Where do you want to put your bag?"

She pressed her fingers to her temples. "God, Gray. I don't know. I mean, I do, but I don't know what I should say."

He was in front of her within seconds, his hands on her shoulders. When she dropped her arm, she was staring into his concerned gaze. *He* was worried about *her* after what she'd done?

"Say what you want to say," he said.

The desperately held dam she'd constructed since she'd seen him abducted broke. "I want to put it in your room and not leave your bed for days. I want you to say that this will be all right, that if you were allowed to know me as me and I was allowed to associate with you, that we would've ended up here anyway. I want to say I'm sorry."

He dropped a kiss to the top of her head. "I'm sorry, too. There's not much we can change, but I've come to the decision that I wouldn't want to anyway."

"Really?"

He brushed a tear from her cheek. She hadn't known she'd been crying. "Really. I haven't met anyone since Lillian that made me wish I could spend my life with them. You know about me." Unease infused his eyes.

"Are you worried about that?" She looped her hands around his wrists. "Because I'm not. You won't be miraculously healed, but you did do well after they tampered with your mind, so..."

"So maybe all I needed was a memory wipe?" His eyes crinkled at the corners.

She smiled. The ice between them broke and the comfort that she'd had with him as Amy returned. "We have shifters who can do what human doctors and their medicines can't. We also have Jace and his power of influence."

"He could talk my voices down on a subconscious level?" Understanding dawned and a grin spread over his face. "This is my wildest fantasy come true." His expression fell. "But you're stuck with me, too."

"Oh, Gray. I wouldn't have mated you if the thought of losing you didn't destroy me." She held up his palm and stroked the mark of their bonding. "I switched hands, you know. At the time I worried that I'd done that because I was afraid of feeling like a traitor to Bane. And that was part of it, but I also wanted you and I to have our own start."

"We'll never overwrite what we had before, and we don't need to. We're starting over with you and me."

Her breath caught. "You're serious? You want to be with me? Forever?"

His smile was a line straight to her heart. "Armana, you captured my heart as soon as you busted down my back door."

He claimed her mouth. She hugged him hard, their lips smashing together. His arms came around her waist. It'd been too long since he'd held her like that. Only a couple of weeks, but too damn long.

He broke away to stroke her cheek. "Think dinner can wait?"

It shouldn't. He had to be starving after all the healing he'd done. Plus, there was one thing he didn't know about. "We should eat first. You need the strength and I need to explain the mating frenzy."

His brow cocked and male interest shone in his eyes. "I can't wait to find out. But I'm not calling the commander for a few days."

She stiffened. Had something changed his mind? Had he interpreted her streak of responsibility as meaning she wasn't truly interested?

"No, I haven't changed my mind. But after having to sneak around because of our kids and because I'm human, they can all sit and wonder for a while. You and I are taking this time for ourselves. Do you agree?"

She'd already be naked if he weren't holding her. "Oh, Gray. I had to walk away from you twice and almost lost you for good. You're finally mine."

"And you're mine."

Dinner would have to wait after all.

EPILOGUE

*G*ray watched Armana as she squinted down the road. Her target walked out of a designer clothing store, one of those that didn't have a clearance rack and offered one-of-a-kind pieces that would devour one of Gray's paychecks.

"There she is," Gray said around a bite of his burger. "How can she afford a store like that when she drives that jalopy around?"

Stakeouts were fun. Each time he joined Armana, he enjoyed it more and more. It was an excellent outlet for his natural suspicion.

"My guess is that her next stop will be a car lot that sells sporty, expensive vehicles," Armana said.

When Gray had called Commander Fitzsimmons and said that he'd claimed her right and proper, all the commander had said was "Good. Now choose a pack."

That decision wasn't easy. Armana's old pack, the one she was technically a part of, where Maggie lived, wasn't a viable option. The pack was in a small village with even fewer options for employment and recreation, especially since he couldn't shift and run in the woods. Sure, they could've made it work, but was that how they wanted to start their life together?

After they spent three days eating and ravishing each other, Armana moved her things into his home, what little she had. She didn't want to leave Freemont and neither did he.

As she and Gray talked about their options and went over the time she was Amy to him and protecting Cassie, the answer revealed itself. He went with her when she approached the commander. Did the West Creek Guardians need a private investigator?

"You two will have to go through training," he said. "You might not be Guardians, but you might find yourselves in another shoot-out."

Armana's brow furrowed. "But Gray's going to stay at the Sporting Warehouse."

The commander came the closest to rolling his eyes that Gray had ever seen. "You're telling me he won't ever go into the field with you? Or that once he has to move on from the store, he won't start working with you, or for us in some other capacity?"

The guy was sharp. Any time Gray dealt with him, the male's innate nature to lead was clear. "Commander, did you know I wasn't upset over the mating?"

"Despite your mind being wiped, and amid all the people in Freemont and West Creek, you found her. So, yeah, I had an inclination." Commander Fitzsimmons pinned Armana with his steely gaze. "And you risked Jace's wrath to be with him. You wouldn't do that for someone you didn't love."

Yes. Jace. He'd been upset with her. Gray invited him and Cassie over and after a tension-filled dinner, the icy wall around Jace's heart started to melt. "You two are really into each other," he said.

"I told you," Cassie replied. "You weren't around to see them together, and if I hadn't been so worried about you and Dad, I would've caught it earlier."

Before they left that night, Armana and Jace went outside for a long and overdue talk. After they left, Armana admitted that it was the first time in years that she wasn't second-guessing herself or looking over her shoulder.

Now she was back out hunting, only this time it was for humans who were working for rogue shifters to sell out both species.

Their target had gone into a jewelry store. This one the Guardians suspected of recruiting her friends at school to parties where they were drugged and used for sex, only to wake in the morning utterly violated with no memory.

While the girl was in the store, Gray figured it was the right time to spill his news. "I put in my notice."

Armana's bright gaze landed on him. "Are we going to be partners?"

"Miller and Stockwell Security will be a full-time team." The Guardians didn't have the time or shifter-power to do what they did: drive around and spy on people.

"M&S Security, I like it." Armana had kept her last name. He had thought it because it represented the person she'd grown into after she'd run with her children. But she'd said that it was generic and wouldn't link her back to a Guardian. His crafty female. "I think we should recruit more shifters. Jace mentioned a buddy at the club he used to work at."

"Pale Moonlight?" Gray hadn't been there, but Cassie had told him just enough about the shifter bar to read between the lines. Carnal desires in a safe place.

"I told him I thought there was a need for bodyguards for human mates when they're away from the pack. Guardians can't cover it all, but it could be a service we offer. Maybe we could hire on his friend Waylon. I think Jace is worried this guy is getting restless, arguing with his pack leader more, and going rogue might be next."

"Any clue why?"

Armana shrugged. "I guess Waylon says he's 'fine,' so maybe if we can keep him busy, it'll either work itself out or"—she smirked—"we'll get to the bottom of it."

Expand the business before it even started? Why not? The summer had revealed some weaknesses in the shifter world, which Gray was now a part of.

He was cautiously optimistic about his disease. His voices and paranoia were more subdued than they'd been in… decades. And he'd talked to Jace. The male was ready with his special ability in case his disease resurged.

Gray and Cassie talked like they never had before. It was the relationship he'd always dreamed about with his daughter.

He clasped Armana's hand. "When do we approach Waylon and offer him a job?"

Her eyes twinkled as she squeezed his hand in return and outlined her plan.

The voice in his head picked that moment to whisper something new.

She loves you.

Yes. He believed it.

DID you know Jace's story was the first book I ever wrote, and that it kicked off this whole shifter world? Check it out. It's FREE!

AND MAGGIE'S story where her destiny caught them all by surprise is the first in this series. Take a look!

THANK YOU FOR READING. I'd love to know what you thought. Please consider leaving a review at the retailer the book was purchased from.

~Marie

FOR NEW RELEASE UPDATES, chapter sneak peeks, and exclusive quarterly short stories, sign up for Marie's newsletter and receive download links for the book that started it all, *Fever Claim*, and three short stories of characters from the series.

ABOUT THE AUTHOR

Marie Johnston lives in the upper-Midwest with her husband, four kids, and an old cat. Deciding to trade in her lab coat for a laptop, she's writing down all the tales she's been making up in her head for years. An avid reader of paranormal romance, these are the stories hanging out and waiting to be told between the demands of work, home, and the endless chauffeuring that comes with children.

mariejohnstonwriter.com
Facebook
Twitter @mjohnstonwriter

ALSO BY MARIE JOHNSTON

The Sigma Menace:
Fever Claim (Book 1)
Primal Claim (Book 2)
True Claim (Book 3)
Reclaim (Book 3.5)
Lawful Claim (Book 4)
Pure Claim (Book 5)

New Vampire Disorder:
Demetrius (Book 1)
Rourke (Book 2)
Bishop (Book 3)
Stryke (Book 4)
Creed (Book 5)

Pale Moonlight:
Birthright (Book 1)
Ancient Ties (Book 2)